THE FISH AND THE NOT FISH

PETER MARKUS

db
DZANC
BOOKS

DZANC
BOOKS

5220 Dexter Ann Arbor Rd.
Ann Arbor, MI 48103
www.dzancbooks.org

The Fish and the Not Fish

Copyright © 2014, text by Peter Markus.

Published 2014 by Dzanc Books
ISBN: 978-1938103810
First edition:

ART WORKS.
arts.gov

This project is supported in part by the National Endowment for the Arts and the MCACA.

Printed in the United States of America

And then it rained.

Then Bird stayed up there in his nest in this rain and he did not come down.

Bird would not come down.

Bird had a house and had lived in a house just like all the rest of us.

Bird's house was a house made out of wood and brick. He lived in it with a mom and a dad who weren't Bird's mom and dad but were the mom and dad of a boy with a last name that was not the same last name as Bird's.

Bird's last name was Bird but it was spelled Byrd with a y and not with an i.

Jim Byrd was his real name.

But we just called him Bird.

Bird Byrd was what this boy was to us.

Or just plain Bird.

No one knew where Bird's real mom and dad were or why Bird did not live in a house with a mom and dad who were his own.

Most of us lived in a house with a mom and dad who were our own.

But some of us lived in a house with just a mom or with just a dad and then some of us lived in a house with a mom and that mom's mom and dad who lived in the house with us too.

None of us lived in a house with just a dad or with just a dad and that dad's mom and dad.

I don't know why none of us did.

One of us boys said that there were no more Byrds, that Bird was the last to live in our town.

I don't know for sure if this was true.

Though I don't know why it'd be the kind of a thing a boy like one of us would make up.

Look up.

See Bird.

Bird built a nest. In a tree. Made out of dirt and mud and twigs. At night he slept like a bird.

When the sun rose up in the sky, Bird sang like a bird glad to see the sun.

Hear his song.

The sky is blue by day, Bird sings.

At night the sky turns black.

There was a time when Bird was a boy just like all the rest of us.

There was a time when Bird, just like all the rest of us, was a boy who had to go to school.

The man who was there to teach us things would call out to us Bird's real name.

Byrd, James.

Bird, just like the rest of us in this room, should have known what to do when he heard his name called out like this: last name first, first name last.

Bird should have raised up with his hand.

But Bird did not do what the rest of us in this room knew was the right thing for us to do.

So the man who was there in this room with us called out Bird's name one more time.

Raise your hand, was what we told him.

But Bird did not do what we told.

The man who was there in this room to teach us things we did not need to know, he stood up from where he sat in back of his desk and he walked to where Bird in his own desk sat.

Aren't you Byrd, James, was what this man asked Bird what he was.

Bird shook his head.

Then who are you? was what this man asked of Bird next. And what's your name?

Jim, was what Bird said. James, Bird said, was the name of my dad.

The man who was there in this room to teach us things we did not need to know, we were taught to call him Sir.

Sir took Bird by the bone of his arm and pulled Bird up from his seat. Sir led Bird by the bone of his arm up to the front of our room where we got taught things we did not need to know.

We watched Sir try and teach a thing or two to Bird on this, the third day of school.

Turn to face the rest of the boys, Sir told Bird to do.

Bird did like he was told.

Bird looked his face at the rest of us in this room.

The look on Bird's face was the look of a boy who did not look like the rest of us.

We watched the look on Sir's face look.

The look on Sir's face was the look of a man who did not like to look at us.

Sir took this look and he looked this look back at his desk.

In Sir's desk there was a flat hunk of wood stashed back there that used to be used to row a boat with.

Sir held this wood up for all of us to see.

Bird did not see it, but he knew it was there.

Touch your toes, Sir told Bird what to do next.

Bird did.

When Bird did what Sir just told, Sir did with this wood what Sir liked to do best with this wood.

He hit.

And he hit.

And then Sir hit some more.

Bird did not wince, or flinch with his face, or make with his mouth a sound that most of us boys would make.

When Sir was done with this wood, Sir told Bird to stay where he stood.

Bird did.

Bird stayed and stood where he stood.

Pull out your books, Sir told the rest of us in this room.

We did.

We read what our books said.

The words made as much sense to us then as a broke piece of wood did to Bird.

Most of us boys would walk with a limp if Sir had done to us what he'd done to Bird.

But not Bird.

Bird walked the walk that he walked.

We watched him walk.

We watched him walk to where the train tracks in our town ran through the town that was ours.

The tracks in our town had all gone to rust.

There was a time when trains once ran through this town that was ours.

We all once saw trains run through our town on the way to some town that was not ours.

But not the past few years.

The past few years no trains had run through this town with the tracks all gone to rust.

Bird's house was built so close to these tracks, Bird could throw a stone and hit a train on its way through our town on its way to a town that was not ours.

No train runs through town these days, but if they did Bird could show you, Bird would tell you if he could tell you, it's true when I said it to you that Bird could take a stone and throw this stone at a train, his house was built that close to these gone to rust tracks.

When Bird walked up to these tracks, he did not cross them.

He stopped.

Then he sat down on them.

Bird looked down at the ground. Picked up a rock that he saw there. Held it like this in his fist.

When we walked up to where Bird was, what we asked Bird was, What are you up to?

Bird did not look up.

Bird did not say a word.

Not for a while.

But then he did.

He looked up.

In our faces.

What he said was, I see I must have missed the train.

Bird stood up.

He walked.

He walked in the tracks.

He walked like he was a train in these tracks.

We watched.

Then we walked like how he walked in these tracks.

No one said a word.

We walked like this till there was no more track to walk in. When the track stopped, we stopped where we stood in these tracks.

We stopped and we stood like this to see what Bird would do next.

Bird looked at the end of the tracks.

Then he looked up.

The sky was blue on one side, but one side of it had gone gray.

The side of the sky that was black, who of us could see it?

Bird's who.

Bird could see it.

Bird knew that night was on its way.

He sat down.

The rock in his hand was still in there in his fist.

There was no way he would drop it.

That night, we watched Bird look up when the night sky got dark.

There was a moon and the stars for us to see that made the sky not seem so black.

Bird looked up.

We watched him look up.

Bird found a tree.

He walked up to it. Stood with his face faced to it.

But Bird did not climb up it.

That was not how Bird got up in this tree.

What Bird did was, how Bird did what he did was, to get up and up in this tree, Bird flew was what Bird did and how he did it.

Bird took flight.

He raised up with his head. Raised up with his arms out by his sides. And to this tree, Bird, he rose up.

Up in this tree the moon, when it rose up, it looked like Bird could reach out with his hand and touch it.

Bird did not touch it.

Bird just watched it with his bird eyes.

The moon, in the night, it glowed.

In Bird's eyes, in the night, in the black of night, the moon, it glowed right back.

Up here, at night, as Bird watched the moon at night glow, the wind blew through the leaves of Bird's tree.

Up here in the tree where Bird rose up to sit in this tree, Bird said to us one day that the wind in the tree, when it moved through the leaves of the tree, when it made the leaves of the tree move in the wind, that's when he said he could feel it.

When the wind would blow like this through the leaves of Bird's tree, the wind that moved through the leaves and made the leaves move in the tree, it made a sound that sounds like the sound that a bird's wing makes when the wind blows through it.

Bird said this to us too.

The sky is blue.

The sky at noon is blue.

At noon the sky is blue like a sky that is blue.

The sky at noon is blue like the blue of a noon sky.

At night the sky turns black.

Black like the black steel of the steel mill in our town where steel used to get made.

Where steel used to be made.

There was a mill in our town, where the gone to rust train tracks came to an end in the dirt, where steel used to get made.

Be made.

The men in our town made steel in this mill till there was no more steel to be made.

Get made.

When the mill shut down, when the tracks turned to rust, these men did not know what else to do.

They worked.

And worked.

It was what they did.

Was who they were.

What they went to, night and day.

Work.

The mill.

Steel.

To make.

Now there was no more work for these men to do.

So some men drank.

Some men sat in the back part of their yards and hit nails in wood.

Some sat back in the back of their yards and stared up at the noon sky.

Some men sat out back in the back of their yards and stared down at the ground.

Some got in their cars and drove and drove some more and some of these men did not drive back.

Some men found work to do in towns that were like ours but were not like our town if there was work there in these towns for them to do.

The moms in our town who called these men Dear or Bob or Fred did what they did, day in and day out, back when the men of our town had a mill for them to go to.

But now they did it, the moms did, while the men looked back at them with eyes that did not know what else to look at.

Look at Bird was what we should have told them.

But these men in our town would not have heard us say it.

These men did not hear it when we said what we said.

The boys in our town who called these men Dad or Sir or Pa, we went on and we did what we did like we did when these men did what they did when they had a place for them to go do their work.

To make their steel.

To get their steel made.

Now these men were more in the house now to tell us what to do and to tell us to go, to get, don't you boys got a place to be, don't you got a thing or two for you to do, if not let us know and we'll put you to work, and by work they did not mean for us to go to a mill to make steel in.

We'd nod at these men with our heads and go and do what it was we could do so that these men and their gray as ash eyes would not burn holes in the backs of our heads.

We had Bird to look at.

We had Bird to walk through town with, to watch what it was that he might do next.

Bird was ours.

Bird did not have a man like this in his house by the tracks to tell him to get, to go, to scat.

There was a man who lived in Bird's house who went to work at the mill in our town where steel used to get and be made, but this man did not give Bird his name.

That man in Bird's house whose last name was Brown did not say two words to this boy we called Bird.

Or when he would say words to Bird what he would say was, Who in God's eyes are you?

What could a boy like Bird say to words like these?

I'm Bird?

Or else:

I'm just the boy who sleeps in a room at the back of your house with no light to push out the dark.

II.

At night, in the dark of his room, Bird would dream of what it would be like to fly.

In his dreams, Bird flew.

Bird flew on top of the trees.

Bird flew through the blue of the sky.

One night Bird flew all the way up to the moon and when he flew through it, the moon, like a mouth that did not like the taste that Bird left in it, it spit Bird right back out.

III.

There was a pole in our town made out of steel that had a flag run up its side. The flag was red and white stripes with white stars framed in a square that was blue. One night Bird woke up and climbed up to this pole's top with a wood match stuck in his mouth. He dragged this match hard on the pole's gray steel till a spark leapt out and turned to flame. So did the flag when Bird reached out with his hand to touch it.

When the flag caught flame its light lit up the town's night sky. We all got out of bed to watch it burn. We stood and looked up at Bird and at this light that burned bright in the night's sky. Bird looked down on all of our town who looked up at him perched up there with the lit up flag and Bird did not say that he did not do it when we all of us knew that he did.

There was a man in our town who wore a steel star on his chest. We were taught to call him Chief. When the flag burned down to ash, Chief called up to Bird to climb back down, then Chief told the rest of our town to go back home to our beds.

Most of us did. But there were a few of us who did not go, who hid out in the steel cans on the street where trash and things of no use, things that had broke, were thrown in by our town's hands.

Our eyes looked up from where we hid to see and hear Chief call up to Bird come on down.

When Bird came down, he did not fly down like a bird. What Bird did was, just like Chief told him, he climbed. One hand at a time, Bird climbed down from this gray pole where this flag of red and blue and white once flew in the dark that was night.

Chief took Bird by his hands and jerked them in back of Bird's back. Boy, you come with me, Chief told Bird, and he walked with Bird's cuffed hands to the place in our town where the drunks of our town got put when things with them got out of hand.

Bird spent the night in this place where the steel bars you looked out through cut the world up in small squares. Bird liked it the way the bars made the world seem not so big. The sky, when Bird looked out to it, was not one big hunk of blue or black, but was now made up of small chunks that were blue by day and black by night and Bird, he saw, could hold a broke piece in the palm of his hand and then raise it up and press it up to that place on his chest where he knew was his heart.

We did not see or hear from Bird for three days, but when Bird did show his face back at school he held, in the palm of his hand, not a piece of the sky, not a hunk of his heart: no, what Bird held out for all of us boys to see, there in his hand, was a bird that was as blue as the sky.

This bird in the palm of Bird's hand, this bird that was as blue as the noon sky, it had a wing that was broke.

This bird, with its wing like this, it could not up to a tree fly.

Bird would not let us touch it when we asked him could we touch it.

Bird held it up close to his heart.

When the bell rang for school to start, Bird put this bird in his desk so that Sir would not see it.

Once in a while the bird would make bird sounds with its mouth, chirps and cheeps and cawed bird cries, and when it did, Sir would turn back to face us and then he would ask us, What's that sound? Which one of you thinks he's a bird?

Sir looked right at Bird when he said what he did and what Bird did was this.

Bird stood up at his desk. Then he made his mouth in the shape of an O.

When Bird did this with his mouth, the bird in Bird's desk chirped just like a bird trapped in a desk.

Sir looked back at Bird and with his eyes cut at Bird Sir told Bird to stand where he was till it was time for us all to break for lunch.

When the rest of us boys got to go to the room in our school where lunch was served to us, Sir told Bird to stand with his head pressed up to the black slate where Sir wrote down the words and the dates and the names of those things that Sir thought he was there to teach us.

When Bird turned back to face us at the end of that day, his face was chalked white with dust.

All the while that Sir had taught us the words and the dates and the names of those things that we did not need to know, the bird in Bird's desk did not make a sound.

It did not sing.

We all thought it had gone to sleep.

But the bird in Bird's desk, when one of us boys looked in Bird's desk to see it, it was not there.

It had gone, was what we all thought.

It had flown the coop.

But we were boys wrong to think this.

The bird in Bird's desk, the bird with the broke wing that Bird had brought with him to school that day, when Bird turned to face us all at the end of this day, when Bird stood with his mouth in the shape of an O, there was the bird, as blue as the sky, it looked out at us from the O of Bird's mouth.

And when the bell rang to end the day, the bird in Bird's mouth, it opened its mouth to sing.

It sung.

IV.

We were at school with Sir the man who taught us things we did not need to know when this new boy walked in the room and told Sir and us all his name when Sir asked this boy what it was.

This new boy's last name was Crane, Bill Crane, so he sat in the desk right in the back of where Bird sat. It did not take all of us long to see that this boy Bill Crane was not the kind of a boy you'd want to have sit in the seat that is the seat that is right in the back of you. He liked to spit what it was that he'd put in his mouth and hit Bird on the back of the head with it.

Bird did not turn back his head to face his face at this boy to see what it was that he spat at him.

Bird took it, to the back of his head, till this boy could see that Bird was not the kind of a boy who would turn back with his head and spit back with his mouth or hit back at this boy with his fists.

When school let out this boy who liked to spit things at the back of Bird's head, he told us to call him Dog.

If you don't call me Dog, he said, though he did not have to say more. He had a look in his eyes that told us to do what he said, that this kid Crane was not a boy to mess with.

So we called him Dog. He was new. He had a look in his eyes. We'll give you a shot, we said with our heads, not with our mouths, to see if you can live up to your name.

V.

When Bird was a boy not as big as the boy he was now, back when Bird was not yet the name he'd get called by back when he was just plain Jim or James (if you were like the man whose job it was to teach Bird things he did not need to know), back then when Bird was just plain Jim or James, Bird liked to look with his eyes all day long up at the sky, to watch the birds, to watch the birds give shape to the blue that was up there to see.

One look in Bird's blue as sky eyes and you could see that Bird had it in his boy head that if he could he'd one day like to learn how to fly. But what kind of a school would a boy have to go to to learn how to fly like how a bird knew how to do it?

Men like Sir who taught boys like Bird things that boys like us did not need to know did not teach in his school's room how a boy like Bird could one day be a bird like a bird in the sky. So Bird knew, he learned this much from men like Sir, that he'd have to learn how to be like a bird in the sky, not a bird in some room, but a bird up in a tree which is where most birds spent most of their time when they weren't in flight: not in some room in some school for boys but up in trees where the blue of the sky was like a lake that, like fish, birds swam through it when they were a bird in flight.

There was a tree in our town that was as big as a tree can get to be in a town like ours. It was so big, this tree, that when we stood down at the trunk of it and looked up to see what was up in this tree, or up at its tree's top, we could not see up to its top. This tree, it was all trunk, is what we'd like you to see, for as far as our eyes could see up it.

One day, up in this tree, though we could not see him, Bird called down to us boys from up in the top of this tree. We did not know it was Bird till one of us looked up to see the top of this tree as it moved in the wind like a hand that waved down to us. It could have been just the wind, we knew, up there at the top of this tree that made the top of this tree sway the way that it made it. It could have been just some bird, not our Bird, as it cawed out at the sky from its top of the tree nest.

But no, this was not just some bird that made the top of this tree move back and forth like it did this.

This was Bird, we knew this in our hearts, though it was hard for us to hear what he said when he said it.

Bird called out to us and he kept on with these sounds that he cried out as if to say, Look out.

We looked up, not out.

Bird cried out but we kept on with our looks looked up.

That's when we saw what we saw.

We saw Bird.

We saw Bird jump.

He held out his arms out by his side to hug all the blue up in his arms.

Like this, with the blue held in his arms, Bird flew out and up to take hold of the blue that was the sky's blue sky.

The wind, for a while, held Bird up in it.

The blue, for a while, held Bird up in it.

The sky, for a while, held Bird up in it.

But then it let Bird go.

The wind, the blue, the sky.

Bird fell.

As Bird fell, he did not move his arms to try to make him fly. Bird held his arms straight out by his sides. Like this, Bird dropped like a big drop of rain that fell from the sky's blue sky.

Most of us closed our eyes.

Some of us ran so as not to get hit.

When Bird hit the ground, face first to the dirt, Bird did not die the way we thought that he would.

Bird got back up is what Bird did. He rubbed his head. He brushed the dirt and the dust from his hands.

Bird looked us then all in our eyes.

What we said to Bird then was, We thought you were a bird?

When Bird spoke, he spit out two of his front teeth.

I am, Bird said.

I'm a bird in the sky.

A bird in a tree, Bird chirped.

We thought you'd be dead, some of us said, when you fell the way that you did.

Some of us said, We could not look up to see it.

One of us then asked, Why'd you do it? Why'd you jump and choose not to fly?

I had to know how it would feel, Bird said, to fall and not have the sky be there to hold me up in it.

I'm a bird, Bird told us. I'm not an egg, Bird said, that breaks when all you do is drop it.

❖

The birds in our town, when they'd see Bird perched up in a tree, or up on a pole, they saw Bird, not as just some boy up in a tree, they saw him for what he was, as one of them: a bird. Who or what else but a bird, or a cat, would sit perched up in a tree?

But there was this one bird in our town that did not see bird eye to bird eye with most of these birds. This one bird with a stripe of red that ran down its bird head, this bird saw Bird as what he once was: a boy and not a bird. This bird cawed at Bird to get, to go, to fly, to leave, back down from this, its tree. Bird looked at this bird in its black bird eye, but Bird did not want to fight it. But Bird did not want to leave. Bird did not want to be seen, by this bird, to be not a bird. So Bird and this bird that did not see Bird to be what he was to the rest of us boys—a bird—they fought. This bird took a peck at Bird's left eye. This bird bit down hard on the tip of Bird's nose. Bird did not bite, but Bird fought back. Bird took hold of this bird by its black bird wing and he pulled back on it twice till the wing pulled loose from its bone. Bird held this bird wing in his hand and looked at it for what it was. He did not know what to do with it, this wing, though he knew he should make some use of it. He looked at it some more. Then he held his mouth in the shape of an O, but no, this time, Bird did not sing. What Bird did, with this wing in his hand, when he held his mouth in the shape of an O (though he did not with his mouth sing), he took this wing, he brought it up to his mouth, and then like this he ate it.

VI.

One day the boys in our town took some fur from some things that we found run down dead on the side of the road, this road that runs its way through and out of our town, and we stuck this fur with dirt and mud so that it stuck to the skin on Bird's back. The fur, we thought, would make Bird look more like a bird and less like a boy and this would help him to fly. We took dirt and mud and mixed in the fur with it—black and white and brown, all mixed to make a shade like the sky at dawn when the birds like to wake up and sing—till it stuck to the skin on Bird's back. The fur, it did, it made Bird look more like a bird than he did when he did not have fur stuck with mud and dirt to the skin on his back. Some of us boys said, so that Bird could not hear it, that Bird looked more like a dog—a dead dog run down on the side of a road— than he did like a bird, but if you want to know the truth, what Bird looked most of all like was like a boy who had the fur of some dead things stuck, with mud and with dirt, to the skin on the back of his boy back.

One day Bird came to school with twigs and leaves and bits of bark stuck to the clothes on his back. It looked as if he'd had a fight with a tree and the tree was what won out.

The next day Bird came to school wet from head to foot as if he got caught in the rain.

It had not rained for three weeks, not a drop. The grass in our town had all turned to dirt.

Sir gave Bird a rag that was used to wipe the black slate that Sir wrote on in chalk all of those things that boys like us did not need to know and then Sir told Bird who the past two days had been late for school to dry his head and his hands off. Bird took it, the rag, and held it in his hand. What we thought was rain dripped off of Bird's head and back and pooled there at his bare feet.

The sea, the sea, the sea, the sea.

This was the word and the sound that Bird made with his mouth, more than just once, though he said it so low Sir could not hear it.

Where, do tell, are your shoes? Sir said this to Bird when he saw what we saw too.

This school, Sir said to Bird, it is not some barn. I'm not here to teach you how to milk cows.

A few of us laughed when Sir said what he did. Those of us who did not laugh gave those who did looks.

The sea, the sea, Bird said, to make it now six times that Bird had said these sea words, though once more Sir did not hear it.

The rest of us in class did not know what to make of what or why Bird said what he did.

What did Bird mean when he said what he said: The sea, the sea, the sea.

What did boys like us know of that place called the sea? The sea was not the kind of a place that boys like us had been to see.

The road out of town, we'd been told, by Sir and by men like Sir who were here to teach us those things that we did not need to know, if you took it as far as it will go, we got told, it ends up at the sea.

That much we knew.

We'd been told what got told.

But we knew, too, that there was more for us to know of a place such as the sea than just this.

The sea was a big place, this we knew, as big as the sky, a place too big for eyes like ours to see it with just one look.

When we'd close our eyes to see it, what we'd see was a place like the sky, it was as blue as the sky, a blue for boys like us, in our eyes, to swim in.

It took Bird all day for him to say to us, when he could, what it was that he had to say.

The sea, Bird said, his skin gone white where the rain had been on it. It is time to go see the sea.

Bird sang out, so loud this time so Sir too could hear it, It is time to go see the sea.

When Sir heard Bird say that it was time to go see the sea, Sir turned to us and told us, In your dreams you will see the sea.

Sir was right.

That night, each one of us boys, we dreamed we were at the sea. We stood at the sea's edge and looked out and looked up: at the sky, at the black. The moon in this sky was a fish.

We fished.

We caught fish that, when we touched them, when we took out the hooks, they all turned, in our hands, to stars.

This fire did not burn us.

But the stars in our hands left their mark.

We took this as a sign.

At school, the next day, we each of us held out our hands for each of us to see.

We each of us said, Last night I had a dream.

We were boys who did not talk of our dreams.

We were not boys who made much of the dreams that we dreamed.

Bird was the one boy of us who did, who dreamed.

Bird's dream was, we knew, to fly.

And so he flew.

Bird flew to see the sea.

Bird dreamed this dream for us.

Bird dreamed this dream with us.

To the sea, we knew, Bird would take us.

We just had to find out where he was. Bird was not at school that day. When we looked in all the trees that Bird liked to sit in, Bird was not perched up in the trees where we looked up to find him.

When we found Bird, where we found Bird, Bird was on the ground with his legs crossed at the knees.

Bird, we said. Bird.

We said, We all dreamed the same dream.

And then one by one we told him the dream.

We held out our hands so that Bird could see what the stars had left in our hands.

Bird looked up at us with his bird eyes that liked to look through what they looked at.

Then Bird held out his hands for us to see.

In one hand, his left, there was a mark in the shape of a star.

In his right hand, with an eye shaped like a moon that looked up at us, there was a fish.

Bird took this fish and put it in his mouth.

Bird bit the fish head off of this fish.

Then he held out the rest of this fish for the rest of us to eat it.

We ate it.

Bird sang as we ate what we ate.

Once we ate, we held our mouths in the shape of an O.

Out of these holes in our heads, no words came out.

There were just sounds.

When Bird heard these sounds, Bird stood up from the ground.

Bird looked at us with this look.

There was this look that Bird liked to look at us with.

It was the kind of a look that felt as if Bird could look right through us with this look.

We wish you could see this look.

We turned back to see what Bird had just looked at, or what it was Bird had seen when he looked this look right through us.

There was just the road that ran its way out of our town on its way to end at the sea.

There was just the dirt of the road with just the dirt of the road on it back there for us to see.

Bird walked out to the edge of this road.

Then he turned and walked out on it.

The sea, Bird sang, is blue by day, but at night the sea turns black.

VII.

Where the train tracks crossed this road that ran its way out of town on its way out to the sea, this was where our town came to its end and the rest of the world got its start at.

Here we stood, all of us boys, and knew that the road ran through us.

In two rows of four boys in each of our rows, we crossed from our world out to see the next.

Our names?

You want us now to give you names?

There's Burke and Holt, Welsh and Locke, Clark and Spur and Fisk. That's eight when you add me to the mix.

My name's Link.

You can call me The Boy Who Lived To Tell This Tale.

Bird makes us nine.

We are nine and there are nine of us on this road that runs its way out of our town on its way out to the sea.

VIII.

The road that runs its way out of town on its way out to the sea, it is made out of dirt and rock and dirt and rock. When we walk, we make dust. When it rains, we make mud for us to cool our skins with. When it rains, we make mud for us to eat.

IX.

We were on our way out of town on the road out of town that runs out and ends up at the sea when we saw Dog. Dog was on the side of the road, on his hands and knees, like a dog would be, though when he saw us he stood up on two legs like a dog on four legs can't.

Look, one of us boys said. There's Dog.

We looked. We saw.

Dog.

So what? one of us said.

It's just Dog.

He's not one of us.

We did not, with our hands, wave at Dog for him to come walk out of town with us.

The one of us who said that Dog was not one of us was right when he said this.

We all knew this.

Dog knew this too.

We looked with our looks back at the road that would run us out of town to see the sea.

Dog looked with his dog eyes back at the backs of us boys.

Dog asked, What are you fleas up to?

We knew we should not tell him, but one of us still did.

We're on our way to the sea, this one of us who said it said, though he too, when he said it, knew he should not have said what he did.

Dog laughed when he heard us say it. The sea? Dog said. There's no sea for you fleas to see.

At the end of this road, we all of us then said, all of us at the same time, we said this to this boy Dog.

We knew, in this, we were right when we said what he did, though none of us had with our own eyes seen it—the sea. And none of us had yet done it: none of us had walked on and on on this road out of town till it ran out at the blue of the sea.

You won't make it, Dog said.

He looked at us with a look that we knew was looked at us to scare us.

We took this as a dare, for us to make it, when Dog said that we would not make it to the sea.

Dog said, What will Sir think?

Sir think?

We did not think of Sir.

We did not care.

We were with Bird.

We did not know how long it would take us, or what we would do once we got there, or what the sea would do with us. It was just us, with Bird who walked with us, and we were on our way to see, what Bird told us, was ours in this world to see.

This road runs through fields that are made of dirt and rock and weeds. There are trees, too, with birds up in them, there are trees bunched up to make woods, but a few of these trees, the trunks of these trees, they look more like they're made out of bone than they do wood. A tree made out of bone, or a bone shaped like a tree? Did Bird see it this way too? Or did Bird see *tree* and see it as a place to fly up to, a place for him to sit in and rest, a place for him to sit and like a bird sing in the dawn's new day?

The moon in the sky, that first full night, it was full and it pulled us, it pulled us to the sea.

The moon, it was a mouth shaped like an O, a hole in the sky that called out to us, in the dark of the night, The sea, it said. To the sea, it sang out. The sea, the sea, the sea.

And so it was to the sea that we went.

We went to see the sea.

We ate when the sounds from our guts told it was time to eat. We ate dirt and the leaves from trees whose names we did not know. We knelt by the edge of a creek to drink from the cold of its flow. The creek smelled of cow though it could have been the air that had the smell of cow in it. Once we ate and drank we kept on with our walk down this road made of dust and dirt that made its way to where the sea was a thing none of us had seen. We went to see it with Bird who was there to take us to this place that none of us had been. Once in a while one of us would say, Bird, are we there yet? Is this what you mean when you say we are off to see the sea? Bird would turn his head to say what most of us knew—that we'd know we were there when, in fact, we were there, where we'd set out for us to be.

❖

We slept in the weeds on the side of the road so that no one or no thing could see us. We gazed up at the sky, at the stars in the sky, and made up things that we saw there. We saw a bird in the sky that was made out of stars, it was a bird that Bird said was God. When Bird said that this bird in the sky that was made out of stars was God, we looked at Bird as if he had just said there was no such thing as the sea.

At dawn we woke up to the sound of a bird with a cry from its beak that made us want to stuff its mouth shut with mud. This bird, we knew, it was close by, hid up in some tree, though we could not in this gray light see it. Is that God, too? one of us said, and we all laughed at the thought, though Bird said, God does not wake us with sound.

Once we woke up, we stood up out of the weeds and looked up at the sky, then we looked our eyes down the road and took off on foot down it on our way to see the sea.

We saw rocks and trees, sky and weeds, a dead dog dead on the side of the road with its dead legs stuck up in the air like a chair that some man kicked on its back but this dog had no man or boy to kick it or to call to it by name.

We saw cars here and there that honked when they saw us and then sped by us with tails of dust. There was a field filled with corn that was more brown than it was green and the cobs, when we broke them from their stalks, they turned to dust in our hands. We found creeks that looked more like just roads that ran off to where there were woods. When one of us pulled down his pants and said we should see if we could bring the creek back from dirt, we tried but none of us had piss in us to give it.

Won't be long now.

It was Bird who was the one of us to say this.

What Bird said, we'd come to trust it. It was the way that he said it. It was like Bird knew. Or like he saw what the rest of us could not.

So we walked on like this to see the sea. We did not stop when night drew down on us. We could not see but we knew what was there: the road that we walked on, the sea we walked on to go see.

The sea, the sea, the sea.

X.

When we got to where the sea was, we stood at its edge and looked out at its dark. The sea, it was like the sky, like the sky had come down to see us. We looked out at the sea's face and felt its breath blow back on us. We smelled the sea on us. We were in the sea's mouth, all of us. We were like drops of rain that the sea could eat up.

Bird told us to close our eyes.

So we did.

We breathed in with our mouths till we could taste the sea with our tongues.

We heard Bird sing, By day the sea is blue, Bird sang, at night the sky turns black.

When he said what he said, Bird turned once back to look at us, in the dark, and with his arms held out by his sides, Bird walked out and walked out in the dark to the sea.

The sea, it held Bird up.

Bird walked on and on like a stone skipped from one side of the sea to the next.

We turned our heads up and then down to watch Bird walk out when it was Dog who walked up, out of the dark, and Dog was the one who pushed us, one by one, out in this dark.

This dark we were told by Bird was the sea, it turned out not to be what Bird said that it was.

Dog took turns and he pushed us, one at a time, out in this dark that was not the sea.

What was not the sea, what was not the black of the sea by night, was the black that was the night's sky.

Each one of us boys, one at a time, we took turns, we fell through this dark, it was a dark that did not catch us, it did not hold us up. The sea that was black, it ate us all right up.

But not all of us.

I was the last of us to be pushed by Dog.

You're next, Dog said, with a hand at my back. You're the last one left. It's time for you, like all the rest, to see the sea as it used to be. It's time, Dog said, to die.

You mean fly, I called out, to this boy we called Dog, and then I leaped out to be with the dark.

It's true, I fell, this first time I tried to fly, but it was Bird who was there, it was Bird who came, out of this dark, to lift me back up, to give me back to the sky.

XI.

That night, we gave each star in the sky a new name for us to call it by. When the moon rose full, out from the black that was the sea, we knew it was ours to name too.

We called it the fish.

The fish that walks on the sea.

XII.

It was dawn when the blue of the sky blew its cool breath on my face to tell me it was time to wake up.

I woke up.

I woke up to a blue that had Bird wrapped up in it.

The sky, Bird sang, is blue by day.

At night the sky turns black.

This is how Bird took flight.

Bird flew up to see the sun.

The sun in the sky held Bird up trapped in its light.

Bird, I said, to bring Bird back.

Bird. Bird. Bird.

I sang this word with the hole of my mouth to see if Bird might sing a song back.

The sun, it shined bright back.

And the sky made a sound like the sea might make when a stone is dropped down in it.

XIII.

When an egg is pushed from its nest, when the egg breaks in half, a bird lifts up its head.

It opens its eyes, its beak.

To see. To sing. Its song.

THE MAN AND THE NOT MAN

First there is the boy and then there is the not boy. The not boy has eyes that are blue and hair that is long and not black. The boy's eyes are not blue and his hair that is brown like dirt is cut so close to the top of his head that it is stiff when you run your hand on the top of it to feel it. You can't see or feel the ears of the not boy. The ears of the not boy are there, trust us on this, but they are ears that are hid by the hair that hangs down, half the way down, the back that is the not boy's. The boy, not like the not boy, has ears that stick out like shrunk up hands that are cupped up and out from the sides of his boy head so that he can hear what gets said in a room where this boy is not in it when a man and a not man are back in this room with the door shut tight but not too tight and there are words in this room and there are not words in this room that move back and forth from the not man's mouth and from the man's mouth and these words bang and shake back and forth from the ears of the man to the not seen ears that are the not man's. This house with this room that is in it with the door closed shut tight like it is on nights like this, it is not a house where the doors of these rooms do not get kicked at and slammed at and hit at with clenched up fists, where the floors do not get stomped on by the boots of the man or by the socked feet that are the not man's. The black boots that are the man's have dried up mud caked up hard up on the

52

backs of their heels. When the man walks in through the back door of this house and walks in through the house with mud caked hard to a crust up and on the back heels and up too on the toes of his boots, the not man tells the man to stop, then the not man turns back to face the sound that the man makes when he walks in the house and then with this the not man twists and shakes a not man fist: take off those mud caked boots is what the not man shouts. The man who walks in like this in through this house like this has ears not hid by dark man hair but he keeps on with this walk in through this house as if he does not hear the not man sounds that the not man makes when the not man shakes and twists her fist like this to get this man to stop. The not man makes a not man hand take the shape of a balled up fist and shakes it mad and mad twice more like a not man can be made to be mad at a man who walks in through the house with mud caked dry on his boots, but here the man just looks and looks right through these not man sounds and it does not look like the man sees what it is that the not man wants him to do or see or hear. What the man sees when he looks as if he does not hear what it is that the not man wants him to do or to see or to hear, he turns and he looks out through the square of glass in this room that looks out on the sky and the no leaf trees that make this house feel too small for the two of them or for the four of them to all of them live here in it. When the man like this feels small, he can't help but think back to those days back when he, like the boy that is his and who he gave to this boy his name (which, like his, is Jim), the boy that this Jim man used to be used to spend his back then Jim days in a boy world that did not need a not boy to be with him in it. But the boy here who is like this man Jim (this boy who is a Jim too) and the not boy who has the same first name as the not man whose not boy name is Jane, the boy and the not boy live in a world that is theirs, Jim's and Jane's, to share and to live in this house with the man and the not man here in it. This boy Jim and this not boy Jane share a room in this house and a bed that is meant to hold not two, not a boy and a not boy, but just a boy or just a not boy, just the one and not the two, just a Jim or a Jane but not the both, or at least not both at the same time. The boy and the not boy share too the same last name that makes it known to all that they meet that they come from the same man and from the same not man and that they all live in the same small house and they, too, like two birds in a nest, once shared a room in the house made by the not man for all the days when the boy and the not boy were not yet born to be in this world. All this time, days and days and days and nights and nights, the not man did not know that there were two of what was in her for the man and the not man to have to name. The not man did not know that there were two till the day not one, not just a boy, not just a not boy, but both a boy and a not boy came out of the room that for all of those months was a room that the not man held and kept the door closed tight on those nights in the dark when the man came home in the dark with a voice that made sounds out of words that did not make sense when the man did what he could do to make the not man make room for both the man and the not man there in the warmth of that bed. Those were nights when the man breathed his bad man breath in the not man's face and made the not man cough and choke and pinch tight her not man face and shake back and forth her not man hands in front of the man's dark face as if the man was not a man made out of bone and flesh but was a cloud made out of black smoke. Oh no you don't, who do you think you are, these were the kinds of words that the not man liked to say to keep this man and his bad man breath out of her not man bed and face. And once the not man made out of these sounds a door to keep the man and his breath out from where it came from, and once the man could see that his bad man breath could not break down this door to let him come in from out of the smoke and from out of the cold that the man had brought in with him when he walked in through the back door of the house, it did not take long for the man to give up with his breath that he breathed in the not man's face and to give up his breath to sleep in that place on the floor where the floor did not creak when he'd lay down on it. And once the man fell to sleep in this place where the floor did not creak when he lay down on it, the not man in her bed would hold the boy and the not boy close up to her, and there, cupped in the hard palms of her not man hands, she would rub to warmth the skinned walls of her house, and when the not man closed her eyes to see the face of what she could not see, what she saw was a lone tree with a hole in its trunk and with a bird up there in it that cried out to her by name.

WHAT THIS ALL USED TO BE,
OR WHERE NOW ALL WE SEE ARE TREES

On blue bikes the two boys rode. At night. Down the street. In the dark. Side by side. Like this these boys made sounds with their mouths that birds like to make at the break of each day. Caw. Caw. Who. Who. It was their song. They sang as they biked, side by side, in the dark, down the street, to go see what they'd sneaked out to see.

See the boys go.

Hear their tune.

Here they come now.

They don't slow down. Not till they get to that place where they've come to go to.

A house.

A girl.

Two boys.

Jane, they call out, in the dark, up to this house. This house is red and made out of brick. Its roof is black. One light burns and shines out at the dark that is the June night.

It is Jane. She stands where she is, in the door, where she looks out through the dark at two boys whose names to her are You and Him.

You and Him live in a blue house with a mom and a dad who call both boys by name.

Jim, they say. John.

Jim and John are twin boys but they don't look the same.

Jim has blue eyes.

John's eyes are brown like the dirt.

There is more to how these boys don't look the same, but for now this is all that you need to see.

Two boys.

Two bikes.

Blue eyes and brown.

A house.

Night.

A girl.

Jane.

Jane lives with an aunt who calls her Sis when she wakes her up to say that it's time for Jane to wake up.

Jane would like to sleep by day.

By the light of day there is too much for Jane to have to look at.

In the dark of night Jane can look at what she wants her own eyes to see.

Jane, like Jim, has eyes that are blue.

Blue as the blue sky is blue. Blue as the sky's blue is blue. It is blue too.

That's how blue Jane's eyes are blue when Him and You look at them in the blue light of the day.

At night Jane waits for You and Him to ride by her red house on blue bikes that make the dark turn on and off like a blue light.

I'm here, Jane says, though she does not have to say it out loud with these words.

When Jane steps out in the dark, there is a light from her face that this light it shines right out.

It lights its light on these two boys who Jane calls Him and You.

These two boys stand up on their bikes.

Jim and John.

You and Him.

Jane steps up and hops up on the seat of one blue bike.

This night it is Jim's.

You, Jane says, to Jim.

Jim does not say a word back.

Jim nods.

But Him says with his mouth, First one to the creek gets a kiss.

With this, both boys ride on, and the wheels on both bikes hiss and hum like lips pressed tight in the night.

This night, Him gets to the creek first.

Kiss me, Him says, to Jane, and he stands up from his bike.

Jane jumps off of You's bike. She runs down to the creek. She jumps in the creek's dark.

The creek's dark is made out of dirt.

Dirt like the eyes that are John's.

There is no creek for Jane to get her feet wet with.

Jane drops down on her hands and knees and Jane takes up in her girl hand a hand full of dirt that she makes like it is creek that she lets splash in and on her girl face.

The boys watch Jane, the girl that she is, play like this in the dirt.

In the dark, dirt rains down on Jane's look up at the sky girl face.

The moon in the sky makes all of this lit up so that the boys can see it when they look.

They look.

They watch Jane look up.

Kiss me, Jane says, to the boys, to the dirt, to eyes that are both like the dirt of the creek and like the sky that you see by day.

Him jumps in with Jane first. He got to the creek first. What's fair is fair is a thing that You and Him both know.

Him makes his lips like a fish. Waits for the kiss. Shuts his eyes to the dark.

In the dark Him sees Jane come in close.

She is like a fish on two legs, born from some place on this earth where the sea used to be but now there is just plain dirt.

When they kiss, Him hears a sound in his ear like the sound a shell likes to make when it's washed up on some shore.

Hmmm, Him thinks, and he makes this word with his mouth, so loud that You too, with his back backed up to some tree, You too can hear it.

We got to go, You calls out. He kicks at the dirt. Kicks at the tree. Looks at the look on Him's face.

He has seen this look more than once in his life and he wants it back on his own face.

Go where? is what Him wants to know. Him knows he has the look on his face.

To the bridge, You says, and he gets back on his bike. You Know Who said she might be there.

You Know Who is a girl that Him and You know from the time they biked out to the road that runs out of town to the town that is next to the town that is theirs and then it dead ends where there are train tracks that run through this town that is next to the town that Him and You and Jane say this town is ours though these are tracks, more rust than they are steel, that have not seen trains run on them in all the years since Him and You and Jane were born to be two boys and a girl here in this town.

There is in this town a bridge that runs on top of where the creek is and it is here that Him and You and the girl named Jane go to go see if the girl named You Know Who might be there.

You Know Who has a real name and that real name of hers is Sam.

Sam is not short for a name that is more like a girl's name. It's the name that Sam's dad gave her and called her by from the day that he learned that he was soon to be a dad.

Sam's dad, whose name is Sam too, thought that what was in that girl who was not yet his wife was a boy who would take his name and make him proud to be a Sam.

Sam, Sam's dad said, and he laid his hand where he thought Sam was, there in that spot where when Sam's mom laid down in her bed she used to lay flat as a thin sheet of wood.

When Sam was born a girl and not as a boy, Sam's dad did what most dads do not.

He turned.

He ran.

He did not come back.

All he left Sam was her name.

You Know Who is Sam's new name in the eyes and mouth of You and Him.

When Sam first told Him and You what her name was, that day when they first saw her out on the road that runs out of town, Him and You, or Jim and John, what they said to Sam was that Sam did not look like what they thought a Sam should look like, and so they said they'd give her a new name to be known by, but they did not know what new name to call her yet, so they have since called her by the name You Know Who. When Him and You say You Know Who, they both know who they mean. The girl who used to be Sam but is now that girl You Know Who.

You Know Who is not where You and Him thought she might be. When they get to the bridge where they thought that You Know Who might be there, all they see is a bridge with no You Know Who by it. So they go. They go on their bikes to a bridge on the cross side of town where You Know Who lives with a mom and a man named Bob who is not You Know Who's dad.

You Know Who's house is a green house with a red door that makes it look like a stuck out tongue on a face if you drew a house with paint that looked like a face. It has a white fence out front that is made out of wood. It leans both ways and is a fence that could not keep a dog in its yard if that is why a fence was put up in front of this house back in the first place.

There is no dog that lives in this house or in the back of this yard here at You Know Who's house. It's just You Know Who and You Know Who's mom whose own name is Pam who live here in this house with a man whose own name is Bob.

This man whose own name is Bob, when he was a kid, he liked to fish, but now in this town there is no place for a kid or for a man like Bob to go down to it to fish.

There is just the creek for kids in this town to go down to it to fish though there are no fish that live or swim or would bite a hooked worm here in the creek. There would have to be the flow of a creek in the creek for there to be fish in the creek and where there should be creek in the creek there is just dirt and the dirt is so hard it would be hard to know if there are worms that live down in the dirt that is more like rock when you go at it with your hands if you want to dig it up to see what is down there that lives in this dirt.

When Him and You get to where You Know Who's house looks back at them with eyes that are black like there are no eyes for this house to look at them with, what they see is a girl on the porch in a chair in front of a door that is red like a stuck out tongue on a face. When You Know Who sees Him and You pull up on their bikes with that girl Jane on the back of Him's bike, she sticks her own red tongue out at them.

You Know Who's tongue is more pink than it is red and like most tongues if you look at them close what you'll see is that most tongues are more pink than they are red.

The same might be said if you took a close up look at Jane. When Him and You take a good look at Jane, they don't see just plain Jane who is just plain Jane. What they see is Jane the pain and what they like to call her some nights as they bike through this town that is theirs is Jane the Pain, Jane the

Pain, they both like to sing out, not just plain Jane since hey, look here: there is more to Jane than just plain Jane might be to eyes that don't know how to look at Jane up close when the moon's light or the street's light is so bright that there is no way else for Him and You to see this girl Jane by. There is just this Jane and in this light she is at times a pain but boys like You and Him would not have it, this Jane, be a way that was not like this.

What is a pain when it comes to Jane is this: Jane likes to play games with boys like You and Him. Jane likes to make boys like Him and You want the same thing, be it a kiss from Jane's lips or else to have Jane on the back of their bike to ride with her down to the place in this town where the creek is just a dirt path that runs through two banks of trees with stuck out roots and grass that is as brown as dirt is.

Jane is mine is what these boys Him and You like to say to the one who is not the boy with Jane on the back of his bike.

There are nights when You and Him fight.

For Jane.

Nights when Him and You make the blood run down red from the tips of a nose that has just been by a balled up fist hit to say in a way that words just can't, Jane is just and all mine.

You Know Who jumps on the back of the bike with Jane not on it—on this night this would be Him's bike that Jane is on—and like this the boys ride through town with the girls with their long girl hair blown back by the wind that the bikes make when Him and You pump their feet back and forth as they bike like this till they stop.

Where and when they stop there is this house at the edge of this town where this town comes to an end and is the start of a new town with a name that is all its own. This house, with no white fence out front in the front of its front yard, it is white and made out of wood. Here in this house there is no one here who lives in it. This house with the glass that is now shut in with wood, it used to have an old man who lived here in it, but it's been years since this house has had this man who looked out from in it. This man whose name was known by all those in town as Old Man Mans, he has been dead for all of the years since Him and You and You Know Who and that girl named Jane have been boys and girls who call the town that is theirs their own. But still it is well known, by both sets of boys and girls, that this old man, Old Man Mans, he was a mean old man, the kind of a man who liked to spit and kick at his dog. That's the kind of man that this Old Man Mans was. For some years, more than a few, that old dog that Old Man Mans liked to spit at and kick, it lived on its own, once the old man died, out back in the back of the old man's house. It, this dog, it had a house of its own, out back in the back of the old man's house, and this house, that was the dog's, where the dog it liked to sleep, it too, it was white just like the old man's house, and it was made out of wood too. It's true that this dog, it lived on for some years more in the white house out back of the old man's house. It lived, this dog did, till one night, it's been told, it ran out to the road that runs out through to where this house sits and it sat out in the road till it got hit by a truck that when it hit it, the man who sat up in the front of this truck, he did not stop or get out or look back once to see what it was that his truck had just hit. It, this truck, it had just hit and it had just killed the dog that once lived in a house of its own out back in the house that used to house in it the man in this town known to most all as the man who liked to spit at and kick at his dog.

So there are times when You and Him walk out back to the back of this old man's yard to fight. Here, like this, these two boys face off and here, like this, Him and You, they raise up their fists. Come on, they say. Put up your dukes, one of them will say. Come on, boy, take the first punch. Both of these boys will bob with their boy heads. One of the boys will make the first move. One boy will spit at, then kick at, the dirt. One boy will thumb his thumb to his nose. This is the way these boys say, not with their words, I'm tough.

Then, like this, they fight. They throw a punch or three or four and stick a thumb in one boy's eye. You and Him, they do not wince or flinch or make a sound with their boy mouths when they hit like this with their fists. They fight, they spit, they lick at their lips till one of these two boys says, Give up? Give up? Give up what? one boy will say and he'll hit his own fists bone to bone. Give up, the boy who says these words will say it, the girl who goes by the name Jane. Jane the Pain is how the boys call her when she is not near to them to hear this said. But still the boys fight. They fight till the girls who are with them tell them to stop. When the two girls, Jane and You Know Who who are with them, tell the boys to stop, the girls then turn with their girl heads and look this sharp, hard look at the girl who has just said what it is she has said, and then they stand and stare with their eyes and they too start to fight. They fight like light in a dark sky fights, all flash and flick of the wrists, no fists need to be made for this to be a fight. They fight with the slap of hands hard to hit at a face. They fight with a grip of fist to take hold of a hand filled with hair. When one girl cries out, Give up, it is not to ask it but to say it, as in I give up. Give up what? is what the girl who has a fist of not her own hair in her hand. To this, the girl who says it, who is bent low to the dirt, she makes it known that it is boys which is what she gives up. Boys, she says. Boys. I give up boys. The two boys, Him and You, when they hear this get said, they turn with their heads to face the stars and the moon, they raise up their fists as if to say You, as if to say Him, as if both wish to say, We are not the boys that she means to say when she says it that boys is what it is she gives up.

Old Man Mans, he was a man well known in this town as an old man who liked to spit at and kick at his dog. He was not not known as a kind kind of man, this old man: not kind to his dog, for sure, or to the kids in this town who at times liked to walk on his yard's grass. It's not like this grass was green. This grass, in this old man's yard, it was dirt brown. It was more dirt, this grass was, than it was grass. Grass like this, it was not the kind of grass that is the kind of grass that is not to be walked on is what I want you to see. But Old Man Mans liked to come and run out of his house with his hands made to be fists and he'd curse and yell at the kids like Him and You who liked to walk on the grass that was the grass that was in the front and the back of his yard. You and Him's dad liked to tell of the time, way on back when he was just a boy too who lived in this town where out on the edge of it lived Old Man Mans, of the time when he was nine and he stepped with just one foot on this old man's front yard grass and out of this house, which was white back then too (though the wood was not so old and worn), Old Man Mans who was not so old a man back then, he ran out at him, out at You and Him's dad, out of his house with a gun held out in his hand. Next time you come round here and set one foot in my yard, the old man yelled out at Him and You's then just a boy dad, I'll shoot you off it till you turn dead. Him and You's dad who was just a boy of nine ran and ran as fast as he could run, he likes to tell it, and boys, he says, I did not stop, he says it like this, and he huffs and he huffs, till he ran and ran and ran so fast that he'd run his boy self out of breath. Him and You'd dad, to Him and You, he was just a dad and not some kid that an old man could get mad at, but they laughed and did what they could to try to see it, in their heads, the man they called dad back when he was a boy like them. They could not see this, in their boy heads, their dad as the kind of a boy who had to run till he ran out of breath just to not get shot the day he stepped one foot on the grass that was the yard of that old man who liked to spit at and kick at his dog.

So what they liked to do was, some nights, some days too, when there was not much else for boys like Him and You to do in a town like this town, they would act out the words that their dad liked to tell them when he told them of that day, way back when it was to them, when Old Man Mans ran out of his house at their dad with a gun stuck out in his hand. Him and You would take turns and flip a coin to see who'd get to be the old man who liked to kick at and spit at his dog, who got to run out of the house and yell and curse at the boy who played like he was their dad who had stepped just one foot of his on the grass in the front of this old man's house. To be Old Man Mans was the thing to be since he was the one who got to yell and curse and scream and run out from the back of the house at Him or You or who it was who had to be the son who got to make like he was the dad back when he was a boy of nine. The boy who got to be the old man who liked to spit at and kick at his dog got to make his hand in the shape of a gun and got to go bang and then bang with his mouth and got to say bad words that he could not say when his dad was close by to hear.

There were times too when Jane was with them when she would say, How come I can't play a part too? Him and

You would look back and forth and back and forth two more times and then they'd turn their looks back at Jane. Well who do you want to be? is what Him and You would say to Jane. And to this, what Jane liked to say to this was, I'd like to be the old man's wife. But this old man, he did not have a wife was what Him and You would have to tell her. Well, he's got a wife now, Jane would say, and then she'd kiss the boy who got to be, on this day, the old man who had a dog but not a wife to spit at or kick.

It was Jane too who was the one who thought of it to ask it, one day as Him and You and Jane played at this game that they liked to call it 'The Day that Old Man Mans Pulled a Gun Out On Our Dad," that what they did not have with them to play the game right was a boy or girl to be the old man's dog. Dog, both of the boys said, with a shake of their boy heads. There's no one here to be the dog. And that was the day when You Know Who walked by with an ice cream cone in her hand. Want to play? Jane had said to this girl who would soon come to be known as You Know Who who they did not yet know who she was. In fact, they had not, not a once, not Him or You or not Jane too, seen this girl walk through this town, or walk out near the edge of this town, which is where this house was that used to be the white house made out of wood of the man who liked to spit at and kick at his dog. Play what? was what the girl You Know asked this girl Jane who stood in front of these two boys. It was You who said it, to You Know Who, You get to be the dog. You Know Who was not the type of a girl who would say back to this, But what if I don't want to be the dog? You Know Who's mouth did not make such sounds as this. What she did do was, this You Know Who, and when she did this she did not tell them what was her name, she dropped down, in the dirt, on her hands and knees, and she barked a loud bark at these two boys. It's true: she barked like a dog likes to bark, and then she looked up at Jane, she looked up from the dirt, and she stuck out her tongue out from her girl mouth. And You Know Who's tongue, when she stuck it out like this, Him and You and Jane too, they saw that this tongue, it too, just like Jane's, just like the tongue in Him's and You's mouth, it was a tongue that was pink.

And so they took You Know Who in, as a dog, they made of this girl a dog that they would play with. Him and You took turns, they each got to be the old man who liked to spit at and kick at his dog, and Jane got to be the old man's wife and You Know Who got to be the dog. This is how it went till one day You Know Who got it in her girl head to come up with a new game for them to play. I've got a new game that we should play is how You Know Who said what she said. It's called Two Dogs Who Like To Be One. Him and You and Jane, they all three gave You Know Who a look and it was the kind of a look that said, with no words to say it, tell us more. So You Know Who told Him and You and Jane that in this game that she liked to call Two Dogs Who Like To Be One two of us drop down on our hands and knees and make like we are dogs. One of the two has to be one of you boys, You Know Who went on, and one has to be one of us girls. When Him and You asked why this was so You Know Who just said that this was the way the game was made to be played. Says who? said Jane. Says me is who, You Know Who said back. I'm the one who knows how to play it. Jane stared with her hard as stone eyes in through the eyes that were You Know Who's eyes and You Know Who stared hard right and straight back as if her eyes were made out of wood. Who gets to go first? is what Jane said next since You Know Who did not look like a girl who was a girl on the way to back down. So You Know Who said that Jane could go first if to go first was how Jane would like it to be. Jane said yes, thank you, that she would like to go first, and so she dropped, just like You Know Who said that she should, down on her hands and knees down to get down in the dirt. Him and You looked down at Jane who looked up at them both like a dog who looks up when it wants to be fed and they both said, Which of us boys gets to be a dog first? You, You Know Who said, to Him. And you, she said, to You, you get to be a dog next with me. When Him saw that You did not seem to mind which of them got to be a dog first, he dropped down on his hands and knees down in the dirt next to Jane's place in the dirt. Now, You Know Who told them, and she faced them off so that their faces faced off face to face in the dirt. Now it's time, she said, to make like you're two dogs who live out in the woods. So they did like You Know Who said they should do. They barked. They howled. They growled. They bared their fanged teeth. They pawed at the dirt with their hands. Good, You Know Who told them and she set her hand on the top of Him's head. Now you, You Know Who said to Him, get back to the back of Jane's back and stay there like a dog who's told to stay. Him did like he was told. He crawled on his hands and knees to get to the back of Jane's back. Him sat. Him stuck out his tongue and breathed. Jane turned her head back to see. What she could not see was when You Know Who shoved Him so hard that he came up and fell back down with his head on the back of Jane's back. Him held on tight with his arms to the part of Jane that his hands could reach out and take hold of. Jane fell down face down in the dirt. As if to break her fall, Him's face was there in the dirt by Jane's ear. Jane could feel and hear Him's warm breath come like a June wind in her ear. Him held Jane like this till Jane raised back up with her back. This was how the game was played. When it was You Know Who's turn to fall face first down in the dirt with You pressed down on top of her back, You Know Who turned her face up quick so that her back hit the dirt first and she gazed up face to face with You's face. If two dogs had lips and not just tongues to kiss with, this is what it, a dog's kiss, would look like.

All this took its turn in June. Him and You, Jane and the girl known as You Know Who, they played these boy girl make like dog games when no one else was near to see them. They each took their turns, Him with Jane, Jane with You, You with You Know Who, You Know Who with Him, till June stretched thin and then turned to months that weren't June. A year of not Junes yawned by. Then it was a month of June once more. The sky once more was the kind of a blue of a month of June kind of a sky. But then that June took You Know Who with it. Who knew where You Know Who had gone to. Not Him or You or Jane knew where the girl known as You Know Who had gone. She was just gone is all. Like a cloud that was there in the blue of the sky and then one day it was not. So then it was just the three of them now, just Jane with Him and You, which is how Jane liked it to be in the first place. That was how it was, with Him and You on their blue bikes, with Jane on the back of one blue bike, till the day they saw a girl who looked too much like You Know Who for this girl that they saw not to be her. But when they called out to this girl, Hey, You Know Who, it's us, this girl who looked like You Know Who, this girl, she did not turn her girl head to these sounds. Hey, you, they all three called out to her twice more with a shout, till this girl said back to them Who and then What? Him and You pulled up with puffs of dust that rose up from the backs of their bikes. Where have you been? Him asked who he thought it was the girl they called You Know Who. I'm not who you think I am is what this girl said back. I don't know who you three are. Jane said her name. My name is Jane is how Jane said it. And the girl said back, as if she'd not heard of this name till just now, Jane? I'm a Jane too. Jane? Could it

71

be that there could be two Janes in our world? is what Him
and You both at the same time thought. Him and You both
said this name out loud in the dust that had now gone back
to be with the dirt and like this they looked back and forth at
these two girls. The Jane who had been the one Jane that Him
and You till now had known said to this new Jane, We can't
both of us be Jane. So we'll have to call you a name that is not
Jane, Jane told her. I think we'll call you what you look like
to us. To us you look like a You Know Who Two. This You
Know Who Two, as Jane had just named her, said to this new
name, What's in a name? She looked up at a tree. A tree is a
tree, is what she then said. Call me what you want. We don't
name the sky. We don't say the dirt is but the dirt. We just
call it what it is. Him and You looked at the dirt and it was
You who stepped up and said, to this new You Know Who
Two, You know what? You're right, You said. And so what I'd
like to call you is Girl. Girl, since a girl is what you are. And
so Him and You bobbed up and down their heads and Girl
is what this new girl was named. But Jane said Wait, aren't I
a girl too? If she's Girl what does that make me? You're Jane,
You said. That's what you look like to us is how You put more
of his own words to this. Jane gave this girl Girl a look. It was
the kind of a look that said more than words said out of one
girl mouth could say. What this look said was, You think you
won. But I'm still here. We are not done with this game.

When Him asked Girl where it was she lived, Girl said in a
boat is where she lived. On a boat, Jane said back. Not *on*,
was what Girl said back to this. I said I lived *in* a boat. A boat
where? was what Jane stepped in to say next to all of this.
There's no place in this town for a boat to be a boat on, no
pond or lake to float a boat. The boat, Girl said to this, that

I live on, Girl said, is just as much dirt as it is boat. It's a boat up on land, is what this girl said. Hey, do you three want to go see it?

Him and You and Jane all three of them said all three at the same time, Yes, yes, yes we'd like to see it. We like boats, You said, me and him, You said, we do, when in truth not once had these boys set a foot on a boat. Him did not say a word to this, though with a nod of his head he too said: I like boats too.

What Jane said to this was, Fools, there's no boat in a town where there's no place for a boat to be a boat on.

Oh yeah, Girl said, then come see and I'll show you how a boat don't need a lake or pond for it to be what it is.

Girl took them, Him and You, by the hands and she led them on a path in the woods out on the edge of this town to where her boat was the place where she lived.

This path, through these woods, these two boys, Him and You, with the girl named Jane who kept two steps in back of these three, this path, in this town, not a one of them had set foot on. She called it, this path, this girl who led them on this path through the woods they now walked on, she told them, it was called, the dead man's trail.

Why's it called that? was the thing that You asked.

Why do you think? Jane said from the back, so that Girl would not have to, a man died here on this trail.

Wrong, Girl said. It was a boy, is what she said when she said it. It was a boy who drowned in the lake.

What lake? Him said. There's no lake in this town.

But there was, Girl said back. Where these woods are we see, there was a lake here, Girl told them, where now all we see are trees.

How could what used to be a lake be what it is we see here as woods and trees? is what Jane said she'd like to be told.

It just did is what Girl told her. The lake, it dried up and the dirt and weeds rose up to take its place.

And the fish? Him asked. Where did all the fish go? was what Him said this to all of this. And when he said what he said a bird, it was blue, it flew down, out of the blue of the sky, as if to say, to what Him had just said, My old man, he was a fish.

He was a boy, the truth is, is what Girl then just said, and she did not mean the bird that had dived from the sky. He was just a boy, she went on, but that was all a long time back when he was just a boy who walked out in the lake and he did not come back.

Why don't they call it, You said he'd like this to know, the dead man's trail and not the dead boy's?

What Girl said to this was this: that it's not called the dead boy's trail where this boy walked and this is why: that the dead boy's ghost has all grown up now to be a dead old man with long white hair that sticks out on his old man head and on his face.

That ghost of an old man, Girl then said, he is the one who haunts this here trail that we're on.

At night, she went on, in a voice like a bell whose sound you can't help but turn to try to see it, if you stand here real still, you can hear his feet walk on this dirt that used to be, way back when, the mud that was the floor of a lake.

What you just said, Jane said back to this, is what it is how God looks, Jane said. This girl, Jane said, thinks God is a ghost.

God is a ghost, Girl said this to this. He lives in the trees. He's the sound a tree makes when the wind blows to let us know look up and then like this you will see.

You can't see the wind, Jane said to all of this.

See, Girl said. Look up.

And when she did, yes, the wind made the trees shake and the leafs that fell to the dirt at their boy and girl feet, these leaves, each one, each leaf took the shape of a fish.

The boat that Girl took them to, the boat that she said was the house that she lived in, it looked like a boat that had sunk. This boat in these woods that looked like it had sunk, it had a hole in its side so big you could walk through it, and so walk through it and in it, this big hole in its side, was what Girl did when she came up to it.

In it, this boat, there was a wood chair to rock back in and some rope that hung from its back and a steel pail for you to spit in but that was it that was in this boat. Jane sat down in the chair and rocked back and forth in it and asked Girl if the pail was for her to piss in. Girl did not say a word to this, but when Him asked what was the rope for Girl turned and she told him it was a rope to hang all of her dreams from.

Last night I had a dream, Him said to this. I dreamed, Him said, that I was a fish.

A fish, Jane said from the chair where she rocked. In a town with no lake or pond for a fish to live in.

What's that mean? You said. To be a fish in a dream in a town with no lake or pond in it?

What it means, Jane said, is that what you want is to be in a town that is not the place where you live.

It means, Girl said, to all of this, that you dreamed you were a fish. That is it.

If I was a fish, Jane said. I'd not want to be here in a boat. A fish in a boat, Jane made it a point for her to make, is a fish that is soon to be dead.

Is soon to be dead such a bad thing to be?

Him and You and the girl named Jane all looked at Girl who was the one to say this.

It is, Jane said, if you want to grow up to be more than just a boy or a girl.

But what if what you want is to be a boy or a girl who does not grow up to be old?

Jane stood up from where she sat in Girl's chair. Who would want that? was what she then said to this.

Girl raised up her hand to say that she would want that. And then the hands of Him and You said and did the same.

Jane's hands stayed where they were, hung down like hooks by the sides of her young girl legs. The light hairs there raised up as if to reach out to be touched, to be felt, to be smoothed back down.

I have to get back home now, Jane now said.

Since when? Him then said.

Since you know when is when, Jane said.

Don't you mean You Know Who?

No, Jane said. I said you know when, not you know who.

Who, Girl said then, is You Know Who?

You is who, You said.

What?

You are who, you do, said Jane. You look like this You Know Who. That is who you do.

Says who?

Says me.

And you are who?

I am Jane is who.

Jane who?

I am Jane who wants to be more than just a girl is who.

Girl looked at this Jane who said that she was a girl who wants to be more than just a girl.

Girl shook her girl head at this girl whose name she said was Jane.

What Jane said to this is what a rock might say when a rock looks up to see a tree.

But how?

And then:

Why you?

And in the sky a bird flew through the too blue blue and it too, like the sky that it was blue like, it cawed: who, who, who.

Do not ask what kind of blue the sky was.

The sky was blue.

The sky was blue.

But still you do ask.

And so I'll tell you.

The sky was sky blue.

The sky that was blue was a sea.

See the sky.

That's what the bird says when it caws that sound and that word: who, who, who.

Jane is who.

Him is who.

You is who.

And Girl?

Girl is Girl is who.

And You Know Who?

You Know Who is just a girl who looked just like the girl who is known to us all as Girl.

Where is she now, this You Know Who?

Who knows.

Does You Know Who know where it is that she is or where it is she has been?

Who knows.

So where to now?

Or: where do we go from here?

You and Him and the girl named Jane will go, they will get took, to where it is that Girl will with her take them.

Let's go, Girl said.

She turned, this girl.

She walked.

They watched her back.

Then they got back on their bikes.

Their bikes are blue.

Jane got too on the back of You's bike.

They biked.

Him and You moved the wheels with their feet.

The wheels spun, round and round.

Round and round these four wheels go. They went.

Watch them as they go, as they went: these two boys on their bikes.

Down that road that was made out of dirt.

Up a hill they climbed and climbed.

At the top they took a look.

This was what they saw.

Trees, the woods, dirt where there once used to be a creek.

A sky that was the blue of the sea.

A house not theirs to live in.

A roof, a door, both black.

A bird that was blue in a tree.

Look there.

Girl stuck her arm up and out from where it touched the top of her knee.

They looked there to where her hand said to look.

They saw the sky, the trees, the dirt.

But this was not what Girl's hand said for them to see.

What her hand could not tell them to see was what this all used to be.

This used to be a lake was what Girl told them to see. Here where we stand it used to not be this that we now see.

How would you know? was the thing that Jane asked to be told.

I read it in a book was what Girl said to this. And once I saw it now I see it at night when I shut my eyes to go to sleep. I dream this, each night, this lake that used to be here in this place. At night in my boat where I sit and rock in my chair to go to sleep I float out on that lake and like this I fish for fish in this lake, I talk to fish in this lake, the fish in this lake at night when I sleep, these fish talk back to me, the fish when I sleep and when I dream them like this they sing songs for me to sing. Out on this lake, at night, when I sleep, when I float here on my boat, I look down and I count these stars that I see that shine up from the sky that is this lake.

Your boat, Jane said, has a hole in its side so big it was like a door for us to walk in.

There's a hole in the sky, I'm sure you have seen it, it's a hole that is called the moon.

When she said what she said, Girl looked, with her head, at the blue where the moon, in the blue of the day's sky, it was the ghost of a fish, it was full and like a fish eye it looked down on her. A hole, Girl laughed, a soft sort of laugh, in the side of a boat, it won't sink that boat, not as long as the moon in the sky won't let it.

What do we do now?

Like this they waited.

Like this they did do.

This then they did.

They watched.

The sky that was blue turned black.

The moon in the sky moved from one side to the next.

When the sun took its place the moon did not say a word.

When the sun rose so did the lake.

It was, the lake, the ghost of a dead man.

It rose from its dirt grave.

Like this the lake lived.

The lake took the place of the dirt and of the grass and the trees. It took its lake shape as it found its new place in this place that it used to be. It did not take no from the dirt when the dirt said to it, No, you can't, or when the trees tried to tell it, You don't live here, we do.

The moon, though no one here could see it, they all knew it was there, that it hid like a fish in the new day blue of the lake that rose up to meet and eat the sky.

At night they watched it, the moon, lift up in and be with the lake. Like a stone. Or a fish. It sang its new moon song. The stars did not move or dance, or at least not all at once.

One by one, the stars, all but one, burned out.

The one that was left, it did not fall. It stayed where it was.

It fell in love with what was left.

THE DARK AND THE NOT DARK

It starts in the dark and ends in the not dark. In the dark, when it starts, the sky is black. Though the sky is black, the stars stick out from the dark as if they too are a part of and come from the not dark. In the not dark, the stars take leave with the dark. The sun in the not dark lifts up out of the dark and shines its not dark light on all that it sees and all that sees it shine. The sky, in the not dark, is blue. There is no word to say what I see when I say those words, The sky, in the not dark, is blue. This blue that I say that I see in the sky, it is not just blue, it is not just light blue, it is not just what is by some called sky blue. There has got to be a word out there in the world to say what the sky is when I say that it is blue, but if there is such word, out where in the world, I don't know where, I don't know of it, this word, or where it could be. What is, in the not dark, it is not what it is in the dark. In the not dark, the not dark makes what takes place in the dark and makes it not seem to be what it was, or what it is, once the not dark comes to take its place. This is what takes place in the not dark when no one else is there to see what it is. In the dark, I want you to see, there is the man and there is the not man. The not man sleeps in her bed where the man is not in it and when the not man is not there to be a man in that bed. Where the man is when he is not in this bed is he is in some man place where men like to be. Such a place as

83

this is the place where the man likes to go to drink the drinks he likes to drink. Most nights it is beer that the man likes to drink when he goes off to a place such as this, but some nights he comes home with a smell of what the not man knows is a thing called gin that is the smell of his breath. When the man comes home with the smell of beer and of smoke and of gin on his breath, the not man knows not to wake up. She'll lie in the dark with her eyes shut to the dark and hope that the man will go, will get, will go back out. Out where? The not man does not care where. Back to that man place for all the not man could care. Or just out in the dark where the air is cold and the smell of his man breath can be breathed out in the dark and be smelled by just the moon and the stars and a sky that, when the moon and stars are not to be seen up in it, it is hard on nights like these to see it: to see where the dark ends and where the sky starts and it's hard to tell, in the dark, which is which. The not man knows this: that the man's bad breath can touch the dark but that it will not reach the sky. She is sure of this. She is as sure of this as she is sure that the sun at dawn means that there is where the east is. East is where the sky's first not dark takes the place of the dark. East too is where the sky's first dark takes the place of the not dark. The not man's eyes take note of this on those days when the man is gone and these are the days when the not man has time to stop and look and watch the world go by and the world that is dark and the world that is not dark takes both its dark and its not dark shape. The trees in the dark are not the same trees that they are in the not dark. In the not dark the trees get in the way of the sky's sky blue. In the dark the trees are a part of the sky that is there in and is what it is in the dark. And then there are those days when the man is not gone and the man in there in the house with the not man and in with the dark that ends when the not dark starts seems not to leave from its place. The man in the not dark is dark. The man that is in the dark is the same as the man that is there in the not dark. In the not dark the not man can see more than just the shape of the face of the man who is there in the not dark. In the not dark the man has eyes that are small and a nose that is long and thin and a mouth with lips that are pulled tight to make like the line of a scar. In the dark this scar is used by the man as a kind of a knife to cut through to the place where the not man's skin, it is a hole through which words are fed in through to. In this dark the not man eats of these man sounds that come to her through the dark and she takes them in her and makes them to be a ball of string for her to knit with. In the not dark the not man wakes to a sky that is blue and sits in a chair that is faced out to face the trees that are there in the not dark. Like this she sits and moves her fists and rocks back and forth till in her hands the strings in her hands are made to be a rope. This rope, this not man, she takes this rope and in the room where the man is in that place where he has gone to sleep, the not man takes this rope and twists it and ties it so that it is a rope that is a loop round this man's neck. She waits like this in the not dark of this room for the man and his man eyes to wake up. When his eyes look to see what is to be seen here in this room of the not dark, the not man will pull back tight with her not man hands till the rope goes tight and till the man's man face turns as blue as the not dark's sky.

I.

DEAD DOG SLEEPS

Dead Dog is not dead.

Dead Dog just makes like he is dead.

Don't let this dog fool you like he once fooled the both of us.

Look here.

Dead Dog sleeps.

Dead Dog sleeps by the side of the road.

Dead Dog could sleep *on* the road, or *in* the road, if on the road was where Dead Dog would want to sleep the sleep of sleep.

It has been days since we saw this road we walk down with a car that drove down on it.

Come on, Dead Dog, we say, but this dog does not lift his dog head.

Dead who? asks Boy.

Boy is not one of us.

Boy is just this kid who likes to walk where we like to walk, who likes to go where us boys like to go.

Us boys, we don't like to go home.

We don't like to go home to where our house is, to where it is we live with that man that we like to call Man.

Do not think that this man who we like to call Man is the man who gave us boys our name.

This man is not that man.

This man is just the man who took us in when the man who was the man who gave us our name told us that he had to get, that he had to go, and then he left and we have not seen or heard from that man not once since.

Us boys, we were both of us six back then, that day, back when that man who gave us our names up and left.

Now we are six more than that.

That makes twelve.

That man who up and left us, that man who went, who said he had to get, we think he is a man who is dead.

Or at least he is a man who is dead to us.

Us boys, we don't like to look back.

We don't say or ask the sky why did this man who gave us our name turn his back and leave us.

That was then is all we say.

We are big boys now.

Us boys, watch us walk down this made out of dirt road and watch us as we kick at the dirt of the road and watch us as we watch the puffs of road dust rise up from our worn through to the toes boots.

For us to walk down the road like this is what we like to do for kicks.

Dust, us boys, is what we like to kick up.

Dirt, us boys, we like to take the dirt up in our hands and rub the dirt on and in our skin.

This man that we call Man does not mind it much what we like to do with our dirt.

This man has got his own things to keep his mind mad on like the wife that he took in who does not like to cook or keep clean the house.

Man's wife, we do not call her Mam or Ma.

Man's wife is not so old to be a mam or a ma to us.

This wife of Man's, she is more of a girl to boys like us.

Which is why us boys we like to call Man's wife Girl.

Girl, we say, to Man's wife. Want to come with us boys for a walk out through the woods?

The woods is where us boys most of the time like to go to when we get it in us to get up and go.

We go to the woods.

In the woods there are birds for us boys to throw rocks at, there are trees for us boys to up and climb.

Up at the tops of our climbed up trees we can see all the way up to where town is, to where town used to be.

Town is just this turn in the dirt road where the dust in this road turns west.

When we go to town, we like to take this turn and walk off toward the sun.

One time, us boys, we walked and we walked and we did not stop our gone to town walk till the sun left us to be boys who did not fear the dark that was, we knew, the night's night black sky.

When it got to be dark, the stars shined down a light down on our heads and we stood and we stood and we looked and that whole night long, that was all that we did for all of that night's long.

We looked up and we looked up and we looked up.

Each star, that night, in the sky that we saw as we looked up and looked up, us boys, we gave each star a name.

Not one of these stars did we give the name Jim or John, which is what is us boys' real names.

Jim and John are not the names that we like to say when we need to say hey, look, or hey, bro, let's go.

We like it best when we call out to each of us boys the word Kid.

Kid is the word Man likes to call out to us boys when he calls out to us to come here.

But we did not do it is what us boys all the time like to say to Man when we hear him call out to us this word Kid.

Man likes for us boys to hold tight the things that he can't hold when both of his man hands are tied up and full.

Hold this nail, Man likes to tell us.

Hold for me like this this here piece of wood.

We watch Man smack the wood good.

Good, no, Man, he won't say to us that we have held it or have done a thing good.

All he'll say is, when we are done is, you boys can go now.

And so, us boys, we get up and we go.

Go is what us boys like to do best.

We like to go to where the road goes, though the road does not take us as far as we would like it to go from that place in the woods that we don't like to call home.

Home is where the dust is and dust, when you see us walk on down this dust kicked up road, it is dust that is what rises up from our dust skinned skins.

It was on a night like this when the sun rose up at dawn the next day that we saw for the first time that dog Dead Dog dead on the side of the road.

When we first saw Dead Dog, there on the side of the road, the dog that we saw, we thought that it was a dog dead.

Dead Dog did not make a move, or turn his dog head, or make with his dog mouth a sound when we stuck the toes of our boots up in Dead Dog's nose.

That dog's dead, one of us boys said.

Us boys, we left Dead Dog there for dead, there on the side of the road, and kept on with our walk to where we did not know where us boys would go to.

Not to home was all that we knew.

We walked.

We walked some more.

The sun, it seemed, seemed to walk its walk up the sky with us.

The sun, it seemed, it was one of us.

When we turned and went back the way to where home was for us boys back in the house where we lived in with Man, this was when we saw Dead Dog and we saw it, then, with both of our boy eyes, that this dog, it was not dead.

This dog that we thought it was dead, it sat up on the side of the road and it looked up at us boys like it, this dog, it was one of us.

What those dog eyes said to us boys, when they looked up at us up from the side of the road was, Would you please give this dog a home?

Home, us boys knew, our house, it was no place for a dog to be took to since we had no food or bones for us to feed it but for the dirt that we might scrape up for it and say to it that this dirt used to be bone.

But Dead Dog did not seem to mind it that dirt was all that he would get to eat if he came with us to that house at the edge of the woods that was for us boys what we were told was for us our home.

When we brought Dead Dog home with us to meet Man, we told Man that when we first walked by this dog there on the side of the road we thought that this dog was dead.

Oh yeah, Man said to this. You think that just cause some dog sits up like this dog did sit up that this don't mean that this dog ain't dead?

Us boys, we did not know what to say to this.

So we did not say yes or no.

You boys deaf, Man said to us next, or do you both just got dirt stuck up in your ears?

Us boys both stuck our thumbs in our ears and said, No, sir, there's no dirt in here that we can feel.

Can we keep him? we said so to Man, and we all three of us looked down at Dead Dog as this dog licked at his own rear.

Man looked down at this dog as this dog did what he could do with his tongue and what Man said then was, What could a dog like this hurt, and that you boys could use a dog like this to keep us out of his way.

We said our thanks to what Man said when he said it, though we did not say this with a hug.

Us boys took Dead Dog with us to bed that night and we have since that night watched this dog sleep each of these nights, there at the foot of our bed, the sleep that makes you think that this dog is dead.

But dead, this dog, he is not.

Dead Dog just likes to make it look like he is dead.

But this dog is a dog that lives.

II.

DEAD DOG BARKS

At night, Dead Dog barks.

Dead Dog is a dog that barks at things in the night that Dead Dog hears but can't see.

We think that what Dead Dog thinks he hears at night are skunks and coons and dogs not named Dead Dog who hunt at night and like to paw through the cans out back where we put out our trash.

But the truth of it is, there are no cans out back where we put out our trash.

Our trash, Man digs holes in the dirt out back near the woods and down in there we put our trash and put the dirt back on top the way that Dead Dog does with his bones.

But one night when we hear Dead Dog bark and bark and when we hear that his Dead Dog bark is not the kind of a bark that will stop, us boys, we go out to see what it is that Dead Dog thinks that he sees.

This is what we see.

We see a night that is so pitch black dark that we can't see the trees that we know are out there. We can't see the moon or the stars that we know are out there up there too. We can't see where we set our feet when we walk like this out in this at night dark.

Out here, in this dark, Dead Dog is just a sound whose mouth can't, by us, be found.

Us boys, we reach through the dark.

Dead Dog, we hiss. Hush up.

You know what you're in for, we warn this dog not dead, if you wake Man up from his sleep.

Man is the kind of man who does not think twice when he lifts up his foot to kick a dog in its face.

Once, how could Dead Dog not think of this, Man took up a rock as big as a dog's head and he brought it back down on the top of this dog's head.

When we saw this rock, when we saw this rock come back down to hit this dog on top of its dog head, the both of us boys thought that Dead Dog was sure to be dead.

We knew it was not in us boys to get a man like Man to stop this.

We stood back and tried not to watch.

But how could we not see when we heard what we heard?

We heard Dead Dog make a sound with his mouth that made it sound like Dead Dog was dead.

We flinched and winced and made sounds with our mouths that did our best to tell Man to stop.

When Man put down this rock, this rock, it was a dark dark red against the light dust brown of the dirt.

But through all of this, Dead Dog was a dog that lived.

Dead Dog lived through a rock to his dog head.

It's true that Dead Dog limped to where we could not see him to that space where the ground and the house make like a cave down there where snakes like to go and lay their eggs and on hot hot days they like to go down there to get out from the sun.

Dead Dog did not come out for three straight days from where he limped to where it is a like a cave down in there where the house sits up on blocks up above the dirt of the ground.

When on the third day Dead Dog crawled forth from out of that dark place and barked at the stars in the night's sky to say that Dead Dog was a dog that was back for good, that no man with a rock in his hand can keep a dog like Dead Dog down for long, us boys, we gave Dead Dog our hands to smell and lick to see that we were good.

Dead Dog's eyes were shot with blood and the lump on his head was like a rock that had grown roots in his brain, but for the most part Dead Dog looked to us like he was glad to be back.

And the bark that was Dead Dog's, it did not stop.

At night, when Dead Dog thinks he hears what he hears, he barks like he wants us to know what sound it is that his dog ears can hear that us boys do not turn our heads to.

Out here in this night, the dark, we think, is like a thing we can grab hold of, but when we try, us boys, we look like, we think, if we could see us, like Man looks when he is drunk.

There is nothing for us to grab hold of but the hands of each of us.

But us boys, we do not hold hands.

We both just stick out both of our hands to see and feel the dark.

We are like this with our hands stuck out in this dark when we hear Dead Dog bark twice.

When Dead Dog barks, Dead Dog's mouth snaps back down hard like a trap used to kill mice.

When we hear Dead Dog bark out like this, we pull back our boy hands.

But one of our hands does not come back when we tell it to come back.

That hand is in the grip of this dog's mouth.

When we do pull that hand back free from this dog's mouth, it is now a hand that has no thumb.

This we can feel.

But it is too dark for us to see where the thumb is. All we do know is that it is not where the thumb used to be.

We drop down on our hands and knees to see if we can find it but our hands come up with rocks and twigs and dirt.

The one of us boys whose thumbs are both where they are meant to be says let's look for it when it is light out.

The one of us boys whose thumb is not where it used to be says but I can't go to bed with no thumb.

What, this boy says, will I suck to get me to go to sleep?

You've got two thumbs, don't you, dumb dumb? A thumb is a thumb is it not?

So the one of us boys whose thumb is not where it used to be, that one of us goes to bed that night with just one thumb to put in his boy mouth to help him to go to sleep.

That boy, that night, he does not sleep.

At dawn, when the sun comes up to light the dirt and the trees and the sky, we go out to look for that thumb.

It does not take us long to find that thumb, or what is left of it.

This thumb is a bone in Dead Dog's mouth.

This thumb, it has been gnawed down to a nub of what this thumb used to be.

Give us back that thumb, one of us boys says when we see that nub of a thumb, like a tooth it sticks out from the side of Dead Dog's mouth.

Dead Dog looks up at us and barks and when he does the thumb slips down the back of his dog throat.

We watch Dead Dog's mouth come to a close to make sure that the bone, it does not get stuck.

Dead Dog licks his lips when he knows that the bone is down to stay.

Who needs two thumbs when all you need is one? the boy of us who has two thumbs says to the boy who has just the one.

Just then Boy walks up to us to see with us what's up.

Look at Boy.

Boy lives in the woods.

Boys looks like a boy who is made out of dirt.

Boy was born with a full head of hair but with no tongue in his boy mouth.

If Boy can live with no tongue in his mouth, don't you think that a boy like one of us can live with just one thumb on his hand?

To this, the both of us boys nod our boy heads.

But the next time we see Boy, we ask Boy to hold out his hand.

Us boys, we hold out our hands to show Boy how to hold it.

We hold out our hands so that they are shaped like stars.

Boy does like he is told.

Good, Boy, we tell this boy.

This is when one of us boys goes out back to the back of our house and then comes back with a knife.

This might sting, we say to Boy, and then we take turns with this knife till we cut through the bone that holds Boy's thumb to his one hand.

Boy does not wince, or flinch with his arm, or make with his boy mouth the sound of a boy who might cry out.

Good, Boy, we say this once more to this boy we call Boy.

We start to take our knife to Boy's left hand thumb when Man comes out back to take a piss.

What are you boys up to?

Man's piss makes the dirt turn to mud.

Boy does not grunt or say a word.

Us boys, we tell Man that we are on our way to go to town.

Man turns and tucks his self back in and turns to go back to the house.

So, us boys, we go back to Boy's hand.

We cut and we cut till this thumb drops from Boy's hand loose.

It falls to the ground.

In the dirt, Boy's thumb, it blends in with the dirt.

Come, we call to Dead Dog to come.

Dead Dog comes.

When Dead Dog sees what he sees in the dirt, he looks up at us boys as if to say, Is this here bone for me?

We both of us boys nod our boy heads to say it that this bone is for you.

Dead Dog barks a bark that says to us boys thank you.

Then this dog drops down his dog head and starts to eat.

III.

DEAD DOG EATS

Dead Dog likes to dig holes.

Dead Dog digs holes by the side of the road.

Us boys watch Dead Dog dig.

There is dirt piled high by the side of this road where Dead Dog has dug his holes.

See Dead Dog dig.

Dead Dog digs with his two front paws.

Dead Dog digs like he is a dog that knows there is a thing down there that is worth a dog to dig for.

Hey, Dead Dog, we say.

Dead Dog does not look up from his hole.

Where, we say, do these dug in the ground holes go down to?

Dead Dog digs and digs.

Dead Dog digs down and down.

In a while, Dead Dog is down in the down there of that hole. The top of his head is all of Dead Dog that us boys can see.

Dead Dog does not stop.

Dead Dog digs some more and more.

Dead Dog digs and digs and when Dead Dog stops is when Dead Dog gets down to where there is a bone down there for Dead Dog to chew on.

There is more than just one bone down in this hole for Dead Dog to chew on.

There are bones and there are more bones.

There are more bones down in this hole than Dead Dog would know what to do with.

These bones that Dead Dog has just dug up, they are not the kind of bones that might be bones from some pig or cow that us boys might eat or might have one day ate for lunch and then when we were done with our lunch we might have thrown these bones off to the side of the road so that some dog like Dead Dog or some dog not like Dead Dog might find them, these bones, and then have some bone to chew on what bits of meat, pig, or cow, that us boys might have left on them.

Those bones, us boys, we both think, these are the bones that could be the bones in the arm or in the leg of a boy who looks like the both of us.

Then Dead Dog digs up a bone that we see is the head bone, a bone with black holes where eyes used to be, the bone of a boy that could be one of us.

When Dead Dog digs up this bone with the teeth still in it, Dead Dog looks up at us boys as we look down at him down in his dug in the dirt hole.

Us boys, we look down at this bone that used to be some boy's head.

Dead Dog's tongue, Dead Dog sticks it out at the both of us.

Dead Dog gives us boys both a look that looks like to us that what this look says to the both of us is that Dead Dog has just looked at us like he would like to eat us.

We look back at Dead Dog and we cross our eyes down at this dog to say to Dead Dog, Dead Dog, you best take back that look.

What Dead Dog does when we look at Dead Dog with this look is, Dead Dog starts to bark.

Don't you bark at us, Dog, we say.

Hush, Dog, we both of us hiss.

We gave you a home, we tell him.

If Boy was here, we say, but we do not say what we know Boy would do.

If Man was here, we say, but we do not say what we know Man would do.

Our hands, we do know this, they are balled up to make us four fists.

But Dead Dog, us boys, no, we do not with our fists hit.

Us boys, we are not boys that like to hit or kick dogs.

There are boys, we know, who are boys who do like to hit and kick dogs.

Boy is one of those boys.

A boy that likes to hit a dog when he is a boy grows up, we know, to be a man like Man is.

Us boys, we do not want to grow up to be the kind of man that Man is.

So what we do then so that we don't have to hit Dead Dog for the look and the bark that he has looked and barked at us with is, we take hold of one of those bones from down in Dead Dog's hole and we give it a throw and tell Dead Dog to go fetch.

Dead Dog does like he is told.

Dead Dog, he is a good dog.

When Dead Dog goes to go fetch the bone that we have just thrown for him to go fetch, us boys, we jump down in this hole that Dead Dog has just dug and one of us boys takes in his hand the bone that we know is the head bone.

The skull, Boy might call it.

One of us boys then takes it up in his hand a bone that looks like it must be a leg bone.

This bone that looks like it must be a leg bone, it is as long as the legs of the both of us.

This bone that looks like it must be a leg bone, when the one of us boys takes it up in his hands, it feels like the kind of a a thing that when you hold it in your hands, this thing, it is a thing meant to hit with.

When Dead Dog comes back with this bone that us boys have thrown him, a bone that looks like a big tooth that it sticks out from the sides of his mouth, we tell Dead Dog to sit.

Dead Dog does what we tell him.

Dead Dog sits.

Dead Dog sits and Dead Dog waits for us boys to tell him what to do for us next.

Dead Dog, we know, has hopes that us boys will throw him a bone for him to fetch it.

This is what we do.

We throw it, this bone, as hard as a boy like us can throw a bone like this at the sky.

Dead Dog, we say. Go fetch it.

Like this, Dead Dog is a dog that goes go fetch.

Then, like this, one of us boys says for one of us to hit this, and we throw up the head bone up in the air.

One of us boys takes the bone that is the bone that is meant, it feels like to us, like it is made for us to hit with, and he hits at this bone that is pitched up like this up in the air.

This bone that is the head, it floats there in the sky that is a mix of blue and brown, sky and dirt, and it waits for us to hit it.

When bone hits bone, both of these bones break the way that dirt breaks up and then it turns to dust.

In a cloud of dust made from the dirt, Dead Dog comes back at a run back to where we are both of us.

Stop, we say to Dead Dog.

Drop it, we say.

Dead Dog does what we say.

Dead Dog stops and Dead Dog drops the bone that sticks out like a tooth from the sides of his dog mouth.

Then this dog gives us this look.

It is the kind of a look that says to us boys, What should I do next?

Us boys, we do not say to this dog a word of what to do next.

What we do do is this.

We drop down on our hands and knees, down in the dirt, and like this, us boys, with Dead Dog in the dirt with us, we drop down with our heads and start to eat.

IV.

DEAD DOG RUNS

Dead Dog likes to run.

When Dead Dog is not a dog that likes to sleep, or a dog that likes to dig holes by the side of the road, Dead Dog runs.

Dead Dog runs from the hands of us boys.

He runs out to and through the back of the yard where the back of the yard turns to woods and then he runs out to and through the woods to where town used to be a town.

These days, town is just this bend in the road where, us boys, we walk right through it.

There are days when Dead Dog does not stop when he starts to run this run that is Dead Dog's.

There are days when we don't see Dead Dog for days, he has run so far out to and through the woods and out to where the woods that he runs through takes him.

Have you seen Dead Dog? one of us boys will ask.

We both of us shake our boy heads.

What day is it?

The boy in us boys does not know the name of the day it is.

All we do know is this: Dead Dog will be back.

One of these days, Dead Dog, he will be a dog who will come at a run back to us boys. He will run back to us boys from down the road that runs its way out to where town used to be, or else he will run back to us boys from where the woods is.

That one of these days, it is the day that it is right now.

Hey, Dead Dog, we say when we see Dead Dog come back from where this dog has gone off to.

Dead Dog runs up to us boys and he licks at us on our face.

Then Dead Dog sits down and he licks and licks at his butt.

We wipe at the spot on our face where Dead Dog has just licked and licked twice.

Dead Dog, we say.

Get.

Get out.

Go.

Run, we say.

We raise our hands up to make them to be four fists.

Dead Dog looks up at us boys and then he gets, he goes, he runs.

He runs out back and back to where the dirt turns to woods.

We don't see his dog face back for days and days.

When he comes back, Dead Dog goes and he lays down where the dirt kicks up with dust.

Dead Dog, we say.

Come, we say.

When he hears this, Dead Dog, he comes.

He comes with his head turned down to where what he sees is the dirt of the earth.

Dead Dog, we see, walks with a limp in one of his front legs.

We see that it's Dead Dog's right front leg that is the leg that is the one that makes Dead Dog walk like he is a dog that has walked with his paws through glass.

There is blood, we see, on his right paw.

Us boys, we set to fix it up right.

We pour some of Man's booze that we can see through out of the jug that Man likes to lift up to his lips.

Us boys, we like to watch Man lick his lips when he lifts this up to his lips.

It makes us think of when Dead Dog leans back and licks at his own butt.

If Man could, too, he would, too, one of us boys likes to be the one of us who says this.

The boy who does not say this can't help but laugh and laugh out loud.

When we laugh out loud like this, Dead Dog likes to bark.

Hush up, Dead Dog, us boys hiss.

Man looks out from our house from right to left.

Who's there? the man that he is says this.

Just us, we tell him.

Don't you boys got things to do? he says. Don't you boys got some place to go?

So we go.

We go take Dead Dog for a dog's walk.

Come on, Dead Dog, we say.

We tell this dog, It's time to go.

Dead Dog looks up at us boys as if to say that he's just gone.

Bones, we say to this look.

Let's go look for some bones.

When Dead Dog hears this, he runs with no limp in his front leg to be with the both of us.

His dog tongue hangs from his dog mouth like the wing of a bird that is too dead for it to fly.

We walk to where the woods is.

We walk in and through the woods.

There are trees here in these woods that are dead.

There are trees here in these woods that are like drums when you hit them with your fists.

These trees make a sound.

There are some trees here that make us think of ghosts.

There are some trees here that make us think of bones.

We find bones to things that have, for a long long time now, been a long time dead.

Deer and coon, dog and bird.

We find more bones than Dead Dog could, in his whole dead dog life, chew and chew and then dig a hole down in the dirt to put all of these bones down in.

Where'd all these bones come from? one of us boys will ask the boy who is slow to ask this.

We look up at the sky as if to check the gray for rain.

There's been no rain round here for days, weeks, years.

Once, so we have heard it said, there was a lake out here where now there is just dirt and stones.

Looks like it rained down bones, is all we can say to what we see.

Dead Dog, we then say.

We call these words out, Look here.

We lick our boy lips.

Dead Dog lifts his head to howl.

Dead Dog howls.

Hear this dog sound.

Then look it here.

See us boys bend down to touch the dirt of the ground.

We do more than just touch it.

We bring up bones up to touch our lips and we all three of us, like this, we start to eat.

We eat and we eat and we do not stop till these bones in our hands turn to dust.

V.

DEAD DOG SLEEPS

Dead Dog has got bugs.

Up and down his back and down and up his dead dog tail, Dead Dog is all bit up.

Bugs, Man says when we tell him that Dead Dog's got this itch.

Ticks is what he tells us.

Fleas is one of the words that Man says to this.

Dead Dog gnaws at these bugs and he nicks with his teeth at these ticks and these fleas in his Dead Dog sleep.

Dead Dog can't sleep.

The itch and the bite of the fleas and ticks up and down the back of Dead Dog's back keeps Dead Dog up at night and all through the night.

At night, and all night long, us boys, we hear Dead Dog itch.

There is a sound that Dead Dog makes when he turns back his dog head and with his teeth and tongue Dead Dog does what he can to get these bugs to go live on some dog that is not Dead Dog.

But us boys, we don't know of a dog in these woods or in this town that is a dog that is not Dead Dog.

Dead Dog is the one dog for miles and miles for bugs like these bugs to live on and live off of.

This is not good news for Dead Dog.

Some nights, when we can't sleep, we get up and we give Dead Dog a bath.

We wet Dead Dog up and down with pails that we dip out back in the creek that runs out back of our house and then, with our boy hands thick with mud, we scrub.

We scrub and we scrub and we do not stop till the bugs on Dead Dog's back have been scrubbed and run off free.

The creek that runs out back of our house that us boys dip our pails in and the pails that we dump and wash Dead Dog's back and head with, it is the cold of this creek that makes Dead Dog shake.

But just as soon as Dead Dog is shook all dry, Dead Dog starts in with his teeth and with the nails on his back paws to claw at the bugs that are back to make him itch.

The soap and the suds and the creek, we see, it did not do what we wished it would do to the bugs that live and itch on this dog's back.

So we do next what Man told us to do with this dog when we told Man that Dead Dog has got this itch.

Dirt is what this man said.

We take up in our hands and we fill them up to the wrists of us with dirt.

Us boys, we take hold of Dead Dog by the fur that is not yet dry and we rub him up and down and down to his bit up skin till Dead Dog looks like a dog that is made out of dirt.

Just the whites of Dead Dog's dead dog eyes shine out from all of this dirt and from out of the dust that this dirt likes to make.

Us boys, we cough with our mouths and we rub with our thumbs at our eyes, this air is so thick with dust.

In the dust we stand and wait and watch to see if the dirt has worked the way that the soap and its suds did not.

Dead Dog just stands there with us on all four of his dirt caked legs and we see that he does not turn back with his dog head and reach back with his nails to scratch and bite and claw at the bugs that have bit him all up and down his tail and back.

Dirt, one of us boys points out.

We say this word twice.

Us boys, we look back and forth at the each of us and we both make like we are dogs.

We drop down on our hands and knees down in the dirt and we roll our boy selves round and round in the dirt.

We are boys, we are dogs, at one like this with the dirt.

In this dirt, and with Dead Dog with us, we all three of us lift our eyes up to the sun in the sky, this sun that makes dirt out of mud.

Dirt, one of us says.

Sun, one of us says.

Dead Dog does not itch.

Like this, with our faces turned back to face the earth, us boys, at long last, we go, we fall, we curl up our knees, with Dead Dog stretched out in the dirt with us. Like this, we sleep the sleep that would make a bird up in the sky think that all three of us were, like this, face down in the dirt like this, you too, to you, you would think this too, that the three of us face down in the dirt like we are, that what we are is dead.

But we are not dead.

We live.

We live to kiss the earth.

VI.

DEAD DOG WALKS

Look here.

Dead Dog is not dead.

Us boys, we are not dead too.

We live.

We get up on our knees and we get up on our feet and like this we start to walk.

We walk.

And then we walk.

In the dust and the sun and through the woods to get to where town used to be, us boys, with Dead Dog on all fours with us, we walk.

The earth we walk on is made of rock and dirt.

The road we walk on to get to where town is, it too is made of rock and dirt and dust.

Us boys, we make dust when we, like this, with Dead Dog on all fours with us, walk.

The dust and the road and the sun in the sky, they walk with us to where town is.

We walk to where town is so that we can see a face that is not ours.

When we get to where town is, to where town used to be, there is not a face for us to see that is not ours.

There is not a boy face or a dog face that is not Dead Dog's for us to see.

The only face we see is Death's.

The face of Death.

Death's face.

Death was a man who lived in the town where the road took us to when it took us from where we lived, out in the woods, to where town was, to where town used to be.

It was Dead Dog who was the one of us who took us to the house where Death lived.

Death lived.

Death was not dead.

Death lived in a house that was made out of wood, with a roof and with floors and with smoke that rose up from the hole in the roof where there was a fire that Death liked to sit in front of and with his hands and with his breath he would stoke it.

What Death's house did not have was a door.

Where a door should have been there was just this hole in the wall for us to walk on through it.

Death lived in this house with no door on it with no one else but his dead self to live with.

Death was fat.

Death was so fat that had a door been on the front of this house Death would not have fit through it.

Death was that fat.

Death was a fat man with a gut full of death fat.

He looked like he just ate, like he just ate a whole cow, or a whole barn, or a whole town.

That's how fat Death was.

When us boys, with Dead Dog on all fours, walked in through the hole that was the door to Death's house, the first thing Death asked us was did we think he was fat.

We shook our heads.

Death took his big fat gut in his fat hands and held it as if to keep it so that the fat of him would not fall off it.

Then Death told us boys to sit.

We did what Death told.

We sat.

Death sat down with us too.

We sat down in chairs that looked like they would have a hard time if Death sat down in them.

Dead Dog sat down with us too.

Good Dog, we said to Dead Dog.

It had been a long walk from the woods to the town to get to Death's house.

So we all three of us sat down to face Death.

We did not fear Death.

So what if we were in the house of Death?

We lived, we spent our nights with Man.

We were used to what could take place when our eyes were closed up tight to shut out the dark.

We looked at Death's face.

Death's face looked like it was made out of mud, or like a lump of raw dough that had not been baked to make bread.

The face of Death was all fat.

It was hard for us to see Death's dead eyes.

Death's nose was more of a flap in the fat of Death's fat face.

Death's mouth was a dark hole in his head where Death liked to shove in food through.

Death tried to stand up.

He took hold of his gut and tried to push up.

But he could not get his dead self up.

So us boys, we each of us gave Death a hand up.

Death took hold of us by our boy hands and Death stood up.

Death thanked us for this.

Then Death tried to eat us.

We let go of Death's hands and we ran.

We ran out through the front hole in Death's house and then we ran back to and through the woods.

Just once we both of us stopped and we both of us looked back.

It looked to us like Death was stuck in the hole that was the door to Death's house.

Death raised up his right hand.

You boys come back real soon, you hear, Death called out.

Us boys, we did not say that we would not.

We both knew that we would.

So what if Death tried to eat us?

He'd have to catch us first.

Death would have to come to our house in the woods at night for him to eat us up.

Death, it looked like to us, was a cork stuck in the door that was a hole in the front of Death's own house of death.

VII.

DEAD DOG SITS

When Death tried to eat us, Dead Dog did not get up like us and run.

Dead Dog stayed right where he was.

Dead Dog sat where he sat when Death told us all to sit.

So we get it in us to get back up and go and run back to go back to Death's house.

To get us Dead Dog back.

When we get to Death's house, Dead Dog sits up when he sees us.

Dead Dog, we see, is not a dog that is dead.

Dead Dog is not a dog that Death ate up.

We feared this in our heads that this was what Death would do to Dead Dog when Dead Dog did not like us get up and run.

I'm so glad to see that you boys came back is what Death says to us when he sees that we are back.

Give us back our dog, we say.

Take him, Death tells us.

Death says, This dog's a free to go dog.

Come, Dead Dog, we say.

We say, It's time to go back home.

But Dead Dog does not come when we call him.

Dead Dog sits right where he is next to Death.

When Dead Dog sits and does not get up to go, the fat on Death's face flips and rolls with what us boys know is a smile.

Would you boys care to join me for lunch? Death asks us.

We ate, we say, though this is not true.

I can hear what is in us, what is in our own guts, what is not in there, it growls when Death says the word lunch.

It's been three days since us boys have put food in our mouths that is not made of bone or dirt.

There is a smell here in Death's house that smells like feet.

We look at Death's face.

We watch him lick his lips.

It's your loss, Death says.

Death says to us, It's your choice.

If you change your minds, Death tells us.

We take hold of Dead Dog by the scruff of fur on the back of Dead Dog's neck.

We give Dead Dog a pull for the hole that is the door to Death's house.

Dead Dog turns his head and takes a snap at the hand that he knows that this hand, it is not the hand that feeds him.

Dead Dog looks like the kind of a dog that is fed food spooned out of a tin can.

Death's house, it seems to us, has been good to Dead Dog.

Dead Dog's fur shines black like the back of a bird's black wing.

Hey, Dog, we say to Dead Dog.

We say, Don't you know who we are?

We lift up our hands.

Our hands curl up to make four fists.

We tell this dog of ours, No.

No bite.

Dead Dog growls at us boys to step back.

We take two steps back.

Good dog, Death says to Dead Dog.

Sit, Death says.

Dead Dog sits.

Us boys, we look back at Death.

At Death's face.

Fat face, one of us says so that it is just us who can hear it.

We'll be back, we say.

I'm sure you boys will, Death tells us.

We turn to leave.

We make our way for the hole in the wall that is the door to Death's house.

Death says, with the fat on his fat death face rolled up to form a grin, Don't let the door hit you on your way out.

VIII.

DEAD DOG SLEEPS

That night, we go back to the house of Death.

To go and get Dead Dog back.

To go and save Dead Dog from Death.

We go up slow on the tips of our boot toes to look in through the hole that is the door to the house that is Death's.

We see that Dead Dog is curled up at the foot of Death's bed.

Here, Dead Dog sleeps.

The fat on Death's fat face puffs up and it puffs out when Death in his dead man's sleep breathes in and then breathes back out the breath that is the breath of Death.

The breath of Death smells like feet do when you take off your boots to let your feet breathe at night.

It is night right now and all we can see is a dark that makes us boys think of death.

Of things that are dead in the night.

There are ghosts in these woods that at night make sounds that some folks say are the sounds that trees make when the wind blows through their leaves.

Us boys know that these sounds that we hear in the woods at night are not the sounds that trees make when they are blown here and there and back and forth in the night's breeze.

We have seen, at night, and with our own boy eyes, what us boys know are ghosts.

But we don't call these things that we see ghosts.

We call them Death.

There are nights when Death walks through these woods on the look out for things like us to eat.

When we sleep, on nights like this, we sleep with our arms crossed on top of our chests.

We can feel the beat of our hearts beat and beat hard with our wrists.

When Dead Dog used to sleep by the foot of our beds, there was no need for us to not sleep.

If Death walked in our room, Dead Dog would have been sure to wake us.

Dead Dog would take a big bite out of Death's big butt.

But that was then.

And now is now.

Now Dead Dog sleeps by the foot of Death's bed.

What are boys like us to do?

Us boys, let us tell you what boys like us are to do.

We have got to go and get back Dead Dog from Death.

We have got to go back to town to where Death's house is and we've got to steal back Dead Dog from Death.

Which is why us boys are here right now like we are at the door to the house of Death.

Dead Dog, we hiss, through this hole in the wall in this house where Death lives with no dog that is his own to keep watch with.

To this hiss, Dead Dog does not lift up his head.

Dead Dog looks like he is dead.

Us boys, we know that this dog is not dead.

Don't let this dog fool you like he once fooled the both of us.

One of us boys picks up a rock with his hand and throws it so that it hits Dead Dog right in his dog head.

One of Dead Dog's eyes lifts up.

One of Dead Dog's eyes stays shut.

The eye that sees us, we can see that it sees it is us.

Then it shuts back up.

So one of us boys picks up a rock that is twice as big as the first rock was and we throw it so that it hits Dead Dog right in his gut.

The bones in Dead Dog's gut stick out like the bones that you see in things that sit on the side of the road dead.

But like we've said, this dog is not dead.

When this rock hits Dead Dog right in his gut, Dead Dog makes a sound with his mouth that is a yelp.

Or like this sound is a cry from the mouth of Dead Dog for Death to come help.

Death just sits there like a lump of dirt in this chair that looks like this is the day it is now to break.

Don't break, we say to this chair.

Don't wake up Death.

This chair does what we tell it.

It holds up all of that fat that is this man that we call Death.

On the tips of our toes, us boys, we walk past Death.

When we walk past Death, Death makes a sound with his mouth that makes it known that the sleep that he sleeps is deep.

This is the kind of sleep that we call the sleep of death.

Or so we think.

Death is up and is up on his feet when we make our way back past him.

You boys back for some more of Death, Death says to us, and his lips flick up to form a grin.

We're just here to take back our dog, we say to Death.

Who's here to stop you? Death says to us back.

When Death says these words to us, Death shrugs so that his head shrinks back up in the skin that is Death's neck.

Not me, says Death.

You can see that there's no leash round this dog's neck.

Death is right.

Dead Dog is not the kind of a dog that you have to leash.

Death knows that dogs like Dead Dog have got no need to be chained up on a leash.

Dead Dog is a dog that comes when he is called.

But Dead Dog does not come for us now.

Not till Death says to Dead Dog, Go, dog, go home, get.

Dead Dog gets up and then like this he came.

We take Dead Dog home.

We walk with Dead Dog down the road through town and back through to where the road through town turns to woods.

We do not see a face that is not the face of one of us.

The sky we look up at is dark.

The stars we see do not shine.

There is no moon for the clouds to hide in.

All that we see as we walk through town is the dark that we know is Death.

IX.

THE KISS OF DEATH

When we got back to our house, Man and Girl were both in their beds dead.

Us boys, we both knew what to do with Man now that Man was dead.

With Man, we would dig a big hole out back of the house to put him in and then we'd put the dirt back up on top of him till our eyes could not see the face that was the face of Man.

It was a face we would not miss.

But Girl, the way that she looked all dead in her bed, it made us boys want to kiss her.

We knew we would miss her so much.

So we kissed her.

When we kissed her, her girl eyes, both eyes at the same time, they looked up.

Girl sat up in her bed.

I had a bad dream, Girl said.

I dreamt I was dead, she said.

Well, you're not dead now, we told her.

Who's he? Girl said, and she wiped at her eyes when she saw the dead man in the bed next to hers.

He's dead, we said.

We did not need to say a thing more about Man that that.

Man was just a dead man now.

Girl got up and walked from the back part of the house up to the front.

It was not for her a far walk.

Girl walked slow.

She walked on the tips of her toes.

It was like she walked this way so she would not wake Man up.

We let her go.

We watched Girl light a fire in the place in the house where fires were lit to burn wood, to cook food, to boil things to drink.

Girl took up two stones in her hands and made a fire spark from where the two stones hit.

Us boys, we took Man by his feet and hands and we dragged him out back to the woods.

Out here, us boys, we dug Man a big hole.

This hole, it was so big that when us boys jumped down in it, we could not see out.

We climbed out and then we rolled Man down in it.

Man fell, face down, down in the dirt.

The moon in the sky, from this day on, Man would not see the moon eye to eye.

Us boys, we would see to this.

We filled in this hole with dirt.

When we were done, there was more dirt left than there was a hole to fill it in with.

There was a hump in the earth where Man was laid, face down, down in the dirt.

Us boys, we sat down right on top of this hump in the earth and we watched the sun come up.

Girl came out, to see us, to be with us, with two cups held in her girl hands.

Steam rose up from these two cups and curled up round Girl's face.

For you, Girl told us.

Drink, she said, and she held out to us her two hands.

We each of us took from Girl's hands a cup and raised it up to our lips.

What *is* this? one of us asked.

One of us said, It smells like death.

It is, Girl said.

And just like this, Girl turned back to be Death.

You tricked us, we hissed at Death.

We spit back out what was in our mouths.

You're the ones who kissed me, Death said to this.

When Death said this to us, Death crinched up his dead lips.

Why don't you boys give old Death here one more kiss?

Death shut his dead eyes tight and leaned in close to kiss us.

When he did, us boys, we ran back to our house.

Girl was back in her bed.

She was dead.

We kissed Girl right on her girl lips but she just stayed right where she was.

We did not want to dig a hole in the ground to have to put Girl down in it.

So what we did with Girl was this.

We let Girl lay dead in her bed.

Then we went to where the fire was and we took two sticks and stuck them in the fire till the fire lit up both of these sticks.

Then we went round the house and we touched these two sticks to the things in this house—the wood of the walls, the hay of our beds—that we both of us knew would burn good.

The bed that Girl lay dead in, this bed burned best of all.

We stood in the house and watched the fire rise up to take Girl in it till the smoke got too thick for us to see.

We walked out through the fire, with our hands on our eyes, and we walked back out to the woods.

The sun was up and on the rise now.

The moon was gone in the new day's light.

We heard a bird, though we could not see it, sing out twice.

We heard too the hiss of fire.

We turned back one last time to take a last look back at our house as it got burned up.

When we looked back, what we saw was Death.

Death stood out back in the back of our house with a grin on his fat death face.

The fat on Death's fat face made Death's eyes look like two holes filled up with smoke.

There was a fire that burned in Death's dead head.

There was a fire that burned in Death's big fat gut.

Death held his big fat gut with his big fat hands and he laughed the laugh of Death.

The laugh of Death was like the sound that a dog makes when you take it by its tail and pull back on it hard to get it to come.

Death's fat face got twice as fat when Death's mouth cracked in half with the sound of this death laugh.

Then Death walked in, through the fire, in through the house, and ate up all that was left.